"**How**

The low, resonant voice was a surprise, as was the young, attractive doctor who entered the examining room. He was disconcertingly nothing at all like old Dr. Hillard.

"I've been having some terrible nightmares . . ." Beth blurted, not sure how much to confide in this stranger.

"Hmmm." He perused the medical questionnaire she had filled our earlier. "Do you feel there is a connection between the dreams and your husband's death?"

"Probably. But I don't know what to do about it. Please," Beth's eyes brimmed with tears, "can you help me?"

"Are you a Christian, Mrs. Martin?"

"Of course!" Startled by the abruptness of the question, she answered a little more heatedly than she intended.

"Good. Then you have your faith to sustain you."

"Yes, my faith is very important to me." The edges of her conscience curled a little at her reply. "But I'm tired of *other* well-meaning Christians who give trite answers to life-shattering experiences and spout Bible verses that don't even fit the situation!"

In an attempt to ease the tense moment, Dr. Stewart said with a twinkle in his eye, "Perhaps it's time you considered getting married again."

"How can I help you, Mrs. Mason?"

WINDSONG

Linda Timian Herring

DENVER FIRST
WESLEYAN CHURCH
1300 So. Knox Ct.

Serenade/Serenata
BOOKS
of the Zondervan Publishing House
Grand Rapids, Michigan

WINDSONG
Copyright © 1985 by The Zondervan Corporation
Serenade Serenata is an imprint of
The Zondervan Publishing House
1415 Lake Drive, S.E.
Grand Rapids, Michigan 49506

ISBN 0-310-46662-8

All rights reserved. No part of this publication may be reproduced,
stored in a retrieval system, or transmitted in any form or by any
means—electronic, mechanical, photocopy, recording, or any
other—except for brief quotations in printed reviews, without the
prior permission of the publisher.

Edited by Anne Severance
Designed by Kim Koning

Printed in the United States of America.

85 86 87 88 89 90 / 10 9 8 7 6 5 4 3 2 1

For Julius,
who gave me the keys to my doors
and then walked through them with me

CHAPTER 1

THE COOL EVENING BREEZE brushed the day's heat from Beth's cheeks and moved the darkening leaves of the old hackberry tree under which she sat. It was the time of day when the earth breathed a sigh of relief and began settling down, ready for the shadows to take up their duties. Inside the old house, she could hear the shrill piping of her children's voices, arguing over the supper clean-up chores.

A smile played across her even features. Everything was normal. The smile faded a bit as she realized all really did seem normal—even without Robert. Beth had allowed his place in their lives to be almost absorbed, and, with a flash of guilt, she knew that the pain had dulled a little. The knife-edged sharpness was gone. She closed her dark eyes and tried to will his face back into her memory. It came, like a blurred portrait, leaving an elusive impression of him rather than distinct features. He was beginning to slip through her fingers.

"I'm trying, Robert," she whispered to the stars. "I'm trying so hard to hold on to you, but you're sliding away from me." Two years was a long time to live on memories.

A familiar little voice broke her concentration. "Mom, Cally won't load the dishwasher."

"I'm coming." With a sigh that had nothing to do with her recent memories, Beth rose from the creaking swing and headed for the patio doors. Both children clamored for her attention, pleading their case. Silently she walked to the small kitchen and began loading the dishes herself. It was only seconds until a chagrined Sean stood beside her, helping.

"That's all right, Mom. I'll do it. I guess it really *was* my turn."

"Let's do it together," Beth said. "Sometimes I forget you're only a six-year-old boy." She leaned down to nuzzle his dark hair—a carbon copy of her own.

"No." His expression was resolute. "People say I'm the man of the family now. I'll take care of it."

She took a deep breath and said firmly. "Sean, sometimes people tell you things they think are true, things they've heard all their lives. You are not the man of the family, and you won't take care of me." Her glance was gentle as she added, "I need you to be my little son. You can't be a man yet, and you can't be a father to Cally. You can be something I need more. You can be the son of your father. Someday, when you have a wife and children of your own, you will be the man of the family—but not now."

Relief flooded his countenance, and he buried his freckled face in her skirt. "Thanks, Mom. I tried real hard, but I wasn't sure what I was supposed to do." He lifted his chocolate-brown eyes to her. "I love you, Mom, and I'll try to be the best son in the whole world."

"Well, right now that means getting this dishwasher loaded so we can all turn in." She interrupted his

8

protest. "There are only a few weeks of school left, then we can all go on the summer schedule."

That means not many weeks left for me, either, Beth thought gratefully. As an elementary school principal, she had grown accustomed to the long summer holiday, punctuated with short vacations and workshops for school personnel.

"Cally," she called into the den, "do you have your things out for tomorrow?"

"Yes, ma'am," she piped in her four-year-old voice. "All but my socks. Where are all the socks?"

"Try the utility room. There's a whole basket of them. Take whatever is yours, please, and then put the basket back where it belongs."

With the children finally tucked in bed, the coming night loomed ahead. Beth was reconciled to sleeping by herself now, but there were still some hard facts to face: No strong arms to nestle in, no warm body to reach for, no gentle hands to brush away the cobwebs of the nightmare that had haunted her for the past few months.

Beth was edgy and decided a warm bath might relax her and ward off the night demons. Almost ritualistically, she prepared the water, dumping in a generous amount of bath oil. Then she slipped off her clothes, not taking time to examine her reflection in the mirror. There had been a time when she had reveled in her lush womanliness, but she had buried that part of herself long ago.

The water was steamy and smooth, and she lay back in the sloping tub, emptying her mind. *Tonight will be a good night,* she told herself, *no bad dreams.* And when she became drowsy and limp, she rose and dried herself with an oversized towel. Slipping a modest cotton gown over her short, dark hair, she finished her night-time routine, convinced that this time she was adequately prepared for restful sleep.

But in spite of her precautions, the faceless man

9

was there once more in her dreams, just beyond her reach as she stood trapped on the burning balcony. The heat and flames came closer and closer, and her shrieks for help were met by his silent presence and his outstretched hand. Strangely, she was unable to lift her arms from her sides. And the last helpless scream sent her bolting upright in bed. Stumbling out of the tangle of bedclothes, she made her way to the bathroom to splash cold water on her face, concrete proof she was indeed awake and in her own room.

The face in the mirror was still frozen in fright. *What's happening to me?* She searched her disheveled image for a reason for the nightmares. Living by herself while trying to carry out the responsibilities of both mother and father was a logical conclusion. She was wise enough to understand that there was a reason and probably a cure for the intermittent nightmares. But what should she do to break the terrifying cycle?

Beth muddled through the morning in a haze of fatigue, even the smallest task almost overwhelming her. She watched the dragging hands of the clock on the office wall, waiting for the blessed moment that the hands reached ten, her break time. When the moment of freedom came, she hurried to the teachers' lounge.

Wearily she put her money in the Coke machine, too tired even to be mad when the machine took her money and failed to give her a drink in return.

"I've never known any machine to work in any teachers' lounge I've ever seen!" she grumbled, then rummaged in her purse for more coins.

"Need some change?" asked a tall, angular woman as she joined Beth in the traditional teachers' refuge.

"Thanks, I just found some." Beth dropped the change into the greedy slot, braced for disappointment. The machine gurgled and whirred, dropping not only her Coke, but a handful of coins. She retrieved the cold drink and dropped the excess change on the table beside the erratic machine. "Here's someone else's money. How are you today, Peggy?"

"Fine." She eyed Beth closely as she took her turn at the machine. "But you don't look so well. Everything okay with you?" The can dropped out neatly.

"I didn't sleep too well last night," Beth confessed as she accepted the deep comfort of the couch.

"Worrying about something that's none of my business?" Peggy draped her lanky frame over a chair and sipped her drink.

"No, I'm not worrying, at least not at night. I save that for the daytime hours," she said dryly. Peggy waited patiently. "The truth is I'm not sleeping well a lot of nights." She stammered out the next part of her story. "I-I keep having th-this terrible nightmare." Beth glanced at Peggy expectantly. When her friend didn't look shocked or surprised, she went on. "I really don't know what to do." Unconsciously she clenched the icy can.

"Have you seen your doctor?"

"I don't have one since Dr. Hillard died. I simply can't bear the thought of starting over with someone else."

"Hmmm, maybe you could get in with that new doctor. My husband Mike went to him last month." She took a sip of Coke and looked thoughtful. "Stewart—that's his name. Mike says he's good." Impishly she added, "I'll bet your hormones are doing battle with your enzymes."

Beth laughed. "I hope it's that simple. They probably have a pill for that."

"Beth," Peggy urged, "try to get an appointment with him. You need some help." Casually she tossed the empty can into the trash. "Time for me to go inspire my reluctant pupils." Looking every inch the

11

image of authority, she pointed a finger at Beth. "You call him," she ordered, and then she was gone.

As the door swished closed behind her retreating figure, Beth felt the first stirrings of hope. Peggy was right; she needed to see a doctor. Perhaps he would have the solution for sweeping the awful nightmares out of her life.

It was several days before Beth was able to get an appointment. When she found herself actually walking up to Dr. Ethan Stewart's office door, she felt a wave of apprehension.

She gave her name to the receptionist and filled out the mandatory medical history, passing the remaining time distractedly paging through a magazine. When her name was called, she followed a nurse down the hall to a small examining room. She was a bit intimidated by the modern cubicle, for it wasn't homey or old-fashioned like Dr. Hillard's office. "Slip into this gown, please," instructed the nurse briskly.

Beth accepted the small, open garment and smiled as she thought of all the jokes that had ever been made about them. *This truly must have been designed by a near-sighted voyeur*, she decided ruefully.

"The doctor will be with you shortly." And the nurse breezed out. Beth had explained that she needed a general physical, deliberately withholding the information about the nightmares.

Hurriedly she removed her clothes, racing to get into the open-aired gown before the doctor walked in.

Beth was sitting on the edge of the examining table when Dr. Stewart opened the door. He wasn't terribly tall, but his eyes were the most startling blue she had ever seen. His beautifully trimmed rusty-colored beard and hair provided the perfect setting for those eyes. A generous mouth curved in a broad smile, inviting confidence.

"Mrs. Martin?" his voice rumbled resonantly.

"Yes, I-I'm Mrs. Martin." The voice was a surprise, too. She wasn't prepared for the husky, deep tone. He was nothing at all like old Dr. Hillard. Maybe it had been a mistake to come.

"You seem a little nervous. Was it something I said?" he joked in an obvious effort to set her at ease.

She lowered her dark lashes, hiding the twinge of embarrassment. In moments he would be examining her with those capable hands that extended in beautifully tapered fingers. It was more than a little disconcerting.

"No-no, of course not." She lifted her chin and looked into those very blue eyes. "It's just that I'm not sleeping well," she hedged inanely. She hadn't intended to tell him just yet!

He placed his stethoscope on her chest, listening intently. "Pressure at work?"

"Yes, I suppose everyone has that," she said conversationally. Beth tried to find somewhere to look that wasn't in direct eye contact with the man, and found the top of his head relatively safe.

He gave her a thorough examination, making no comments and asking no further questions. "You can get dressed now and I'll see you in my office. Sally," he said to the nurse standing by quietly, "take some blood for the lab and get a specimen sample."

A few minutes later she was sitting in Dr. Stewart's tastefully decorated office, working to keep her hands still in her lap. *He's very young,* she thought, blushing a bit as she realized that this stranger knew her intimately, and she knew nothing at all about him.

She glanced around the room, trying to read the man from the objects in his office. *I feel like a Peeping Tom,* she thought, *but after all, I should know more about him if he's to be my doctor.* His diplomas told her of his educational background, and she guessed his age to be around thirty-three from the dates on the documents. One neatly framed diploma caught her

13

eye: *Doctor Ethan Scarborough Stewart is a member in good standing of The American Association of Certified Christian Counselors.* There were no family pictures on his desk. His private life was still very private, for the room revealed precious little to give him away.

When Dr. Stewart came back, he settled behind his desk, taking the time to fill a pipe with some aromatic blend of tobacco, tamp it down carefully, and light it. As he scanned her medical records, Beth moved restlessly in her chair. The aroma of burning pipe tobacco usually had a calming effect on her, but as the smoke curled about his head, she felt her anxiety grow.

"Do I need to check my will?" she asked in what she hoped was a light voice.

"Good idea. One should always have an up-to-date will, but you won't be needing it anytime soon unless you get hit by a bus." He closed her folder and leaned back, scrutinizing her. "Tell me a little about yourself." He puffed on the burley pipe, and she found this comforting, for it was the first thing that had reminded her of Dr. Hillard.

"I have two children—a six-year-old son and a four-year-old daughter. I'm principal of an elementary school."

"And your husband?"

She had known that would be the next question and she was braced for it. "He died of a heart attack two years ago. He was only thirty-one." She expected him to make the usual sounds of sympathy that had annoyed her from the first day of her widowhood, but there was no comment. Somehow that annoyed her even more, so she made a trite comeback to fill the conversational void. "It's sad that he died so young. He had so much to live for. But the Lord knows best." She waited for the confirmation of her words. But Dr. Stewart refused to play the death game.

Instead he asked, "Are you a Christian, Mrs. Martin?"

"Of course." Startled by the abruptness of the question, she answered a little more emphatically than she intended.

"Good. Then you have your faith to sustain you."

"Oh, yes. My faith is very important to me." The edges of her conscience curled a little at her reply. *My faith is important to me. It's just a little battered right now*, she justified the half-truth.

Silence hung heavily between them for a moment while he seemed to be considering his next words. She had the uneasy feeling the doctor had slipped from the physician's role into that of the psychologist and now had the ability to read her mind and emotions, leaving her exposed and transparent. He could probably even perceive that she hadn't quite told the truth, and it put her on the defensive.

"May I call you Beth?" His smile was so friendly she was embarrassed. At her nodded assent, he added, "Do you want to talk some more about your husband's death?"

Her guard was up instantly, but she hesitated only a fraction of a second before plunging on recklessly. "Quite frankly, Doctor, I'm afraid you'll give me the canned answers I find so distasteful."

"Canned answers? You find Christians often say meaningless things to you?"

His posture was relaxed and she had the heady feeling she could say anything to this man and neither shock nor offend him.

"Yes. Most of them mean well, but . . ." she paused for a moment, her eyes measuring his reaction, then continued. "I hate it when they spout Bible verses at me. Half the time the verse doesn't even fit the situation." She felt her face flame at this unexpected outpouring of her feelings. "I know I should try to remember the truths behind the words." Once

15

again she waited for some kind of confirmation of her self-chastisement.

"Why?" His face was calm and composed and bore no trace of judgment.

"Because that's one of the things the Bible is supposed to be used for."

"Is it?" He tamped the ashes into the bowl of his pipe a little more tightly.

She stood up in anger. "Obviously I'm wasting your time as well as my own!"

"Why are you so angry with me? I don't think you're a bad person because you want comfort from people, and they give you words you've heard all your life instead."

Exactly! He understood! He had given voice to the unspeakable need that imprisoned her. That people give words rather than themselves—the ultimate impersonal gift. And now this stranger had recognized the truth she had hidden even from herself. Beth had to resist the urge to throw herself into those strong arms, to be held and comforted. Resolutely she forced herself to sit back down and draw strength from the warmth in his eyes.

"I do feel like a bad person because I can't find the peace I need from those Bible verses." Leaning toward him, she earnestly added, "I know them. I even read them often, but somehow they just aren't working—at least for me. They're supposed to be meaningful in times of trouble and heartache." Tears brimmed in her eyes.

"And that makes you angry?"

"No. Not angry. Just sad. Cheated."

"Beth, why did you come to me?"

She swallowed hard. "I came because of the nightmares." She recounted the dream that occurred with variation over and over again.

"Do you feel there is a connection between the

16

nightmares and your husband's death?" His eyes bored into hers.

"Probably. But I don't know what to do about it." Pleadingly she looked at him. "Can you help me?"

"No. But don't look so alarmed. I can help *you* do something about them. When you are able to let go of your anger, it's likely you can let go of the nightmares." Blue smoke ringed his head like a homemade halo in a child's Christmas play.

Hotly she said, "I told you, I'm not angry!" Chagrin followed immediately as she recognized the tone of her voice.

"I'm so glad you told me." The voice was teasing, not sarcastic. "I'll wait for the lab reports, but my initial impression is that there is absolutely nothing wrong with you physically. Because the mind and the body work together like a well-oiled machine, I'd suggest several things: Take up an exercise program—it will help to work off your tensions." As if to emphasize the importance of the next statement, he leaned forward, his eyes darkening with intensity. "I'd also like for you to consider coming in for some counseling on a regular basis." Seeing the look on her face, he added, "Oh, you're not crazy, Beth, but you do have a lot of stored-up anger. You could safely vent it here. I think that would take care of the nightmares." His demeanor took on a mischievous air. "And you might try falling in love with some lucky guy." With that, he clamped his pipe firmly between evenly-spaced teeth.

Beth's lips opened slightly in protest. "Surely you're not serious!" When he assured her he was, she added, thin-lipped, "I'm not ready for that. I don't think I could ever fall in love again. Besides, Robert's only been gone for two years. No, I-I don't even want to discuss it." His expression told her of his sympathy. Fidgeting in her chair, she conceded, "You may be right about the anger. But," she insisted, "I'm

17

certain I can handle the problem without counseling."
Watching for signs of disapproval, she raced on, "Of course I should have started an exercise program long ago."

He stood up, indicating their time together was over. "That should give you some measure of relief, but until you deal with your anger, the nightmares are likely to continue."

Beth found herself vacillating between laughter and tears. Never had she expected a diagnosis like the one Dr. Stewart had given her! It was when he patted her gently on the shoulder in a friendly goodbye that the familiar gremlin of anger tweaked her. But Beth's careful training came to her rescue and she found herself saying politely, if not a bit stiffly, "Thank you, Doctor," as she struggled to make a graceful exit.

"Why don't you check back with me in a couple of weeks to let me know how you're doing?" His manner was quite sober when he added, "Beth, you don't need permission to fall in love again. You've suffered and been alone long enough. You have the right to be happy."

Stumbling slightly at the door, with tears of frustration threatening to spill over, Beth kept her face averted and fled wordlessly.

With the car as her refuge, the dam gave way, and she clenched her hands into fists of defiance. *How dare he suggest I need therapy? And tell me I don't need permission to fall in love!* Her total outrage stole the words from her thoughts.

She conjured up Dr. Stewart's face to berate him, but what came forth was the moment he had gently touched her soul with his caring. The face was not overly handsome, but it was kind, and she had felt drawn to him. *He actually listened to what I said,* she thought with surprise. *But of course that's what he has been trained to do. What I paid him to do. How sad that people have to pay for that natural outgrowth*

18

of friendship! There were no sermons, though, no judgmental admonitions. He had simply listened intelligently. For that, she was grateful.

Still, his diagnosis and proposed cure were shockers. She toyed with, and then dismissed, the idea of going to see him again. Automatically she turned the key in the ignition. *Are you afraid he's right?* Her reflection in the rear-view mirror revealed a tear-stained face. There was no doubt that Dr. Stewart had touched a raw nerve.

As she left the small parking lot, she made her decision. *Dr. Ethan Stewart is definitely one thorn I'm not eager to prick myself on again anytime soon.*

The winding down of the school year meant extra work for the busy principal of an elementary school. The next morning, as Beth walked briskly into her office, her secretary handed her a long list of calls she needed to return.

"Already? It's only seven-thirty in the morning," she complained good-naturedly.

"You'd probably better start with the Monahans," insisted Fern. "They're more than a little upset with our disciplinary actions with their son."

"No, *you* start with the Monahans. Make an appointment for them to come in and see me this afternoon." Helplessly she shook her head. "How in the world do you tell parents their third-grader should be in reform school?"

Fern laughed. "If there's a tactful way, you'll think of it. In the meantime, maybe a cup of coffee would help. Oh, and don't forget you have a meeting with the school board at noon."

As her secretary left to get the coffee, Beth leaned back in the leather chair behind her spacious desk. Here, there were constant problems to solve and children to counsel, she thought ruefully. Sometimes even teachers needed a sympathetic ear or an occasional reprimand. But she loved every minute of her job. It had been a real blessing to be so busy after losing Robert. In the last three years that she had been principal of the school, she had enjoyed many of her contacts with parents and colleagues. Yet there were a few she hoped to avoid indefinitely!

The buzzing of her telephone reminded her that she had a job to do, and she picked up the receiver to start her day.

"Hi, Beth, this is Mike Sayers."

Her curiosity piqued when she heard the voice of the youth director of her church. It occurred to her that Peggy might have said something to her husband about Beth's bad dreams.

"Yes, Mike, what can I do for you?"

"I have a real challenge for you, a golden opportunity, the experience of a lifetime."

"Okay, what are you selling?" she asked, grinning at his sales pitch.

"Our youth group is going to camp out next weekend, and we need a capable, exciting, interesting woman as chaperone for the girls."

"You do have a problem! I'll check my list and see if I can come up with anyone who fits that extraordinary description."

"Ah, you're too late. I already have someone in mind."

"I was afraid of that." Hopefully she looked at her overcrowded calendar. "What are the dates of the expedition?" Her hopes fell as she checked the dates and found only blank squares. "I certainly couldn't make a commitment at this point until I find someone to stay with my children." There—that was usually an excellent and valid reason for getting herself off the hook.

"I thought of that, so I found a grandmotherly type who said she would be glad to donate her time to such a worthy cause."

20

Denver First Wesleyan Church
3440 W. Louisiana Ave.
Denver, Colorado 80219
14 90

"My, aren't you efficient?" Did the disappointment register in her voice?

"Beth, you sound like a trapped rabbit." He paused. "If you really don't want to do it, I'll understand. Personally, I was hoping you would, because you're just what the doctor ordered for those kids."

The sincerity in his voice was irresistible. "I'll help you out," she said with more enthusiasm than she felt. "But you owe me one now," she added lightly.

"Thanks. I'll get all the information to you tomorrow. I just knew I could count on you. 'Bye."

"'Bye." She hung up the phone, muttering to herself. *You knew you could count on your flawless preplanning. I can either grind my teeth, or I can plan to have a really good time. It might not be so bad,* she reasoned, *and I could use a change of pace. I wonder who the other adults are who got roped into this madness?* Carefully she jotted the word *camp-out* on her calendar. Then she grinned at the impudence of the youth director. *He's a comer,* she thought.

That evening at supper she shared her news with Cally and Sean.

"Gee, Mom, that sounds like fun." The wistfulness in Sean's response twisted her heart. While she dreaded the trip, *he* was longing for the chance to go.

"You'll get to go camping one of these days." Once again Robert's absence was a searing loss, and she made a mental note to speak to a friend's father about an overnight camping trip for her son. "It's not too long until you get to go to summer day camp. It's almost the same thing." Desperately she hoped that this twig of hope would sustain him.

His face lit up at the thought of summer camp. "This is the year I get to go? Yea!"

The cartwheel he attempted lightened Beth's heart, and it showed in the grin that lifted the corners of her mouth. "All right, Hot Shot, twirl yourself off to bed now. I'll be in to pray with you in a few minutes."

As she turned the knob of the dishwasher, she mused, "I wonder if he will always be so easy to placate?" She dared not look down the long years ahead.

CHAPTER 2

DURING THE DAYS before the weekend trip, Sean was full of helpful suggestions about items Beth should take along, and soon her list was exceedingly long.

"We learned in school that you should always be prepared for any 'mergency," he explained.

But as she packed, she firmly refused the offer of his wind-up Snoopy alarm clock. "Those girls will have me up before Snoopy even thinks of ringing his little bell." She kissed each of them goodbye twice and headed her small overloaded sports car to the church for the packing of the vans.

Mike met her at the car, his face wreathed in a cheerful smile. "Good morning. May I help you with your packages, madam?"

"First you can help me with the door handle," she grumbled. "Why do camping trips always have to start at dawn? You really ought to let the sun get a good start on the day before you burst in on him."

"I see you haven't had enough coffee yet," he said solicitously. "I brought a Thermos of the precious

23

liquid, just in case." He opened the container and poured a steaming cupful.

For once she was glad of his organizational skills. "Aren't you having some?"

"No, thanks, I never touch the stuff."

As the young man bounded off, Beth considered her chances of the perfect murder, but let it go, knowing she would need Mike on the trip. She sat in her car, sipping the hot coffee and watching the young people scurry around, loading the three vans.

From behind her, a pleasant, masculine voice broke her contemplative mood. She was startled, for she had never expected to hear it here, but she recognized it immediately. "Dr. Stewart! Surely you haven't been roped into this roundup, too!"

"Nope, I volunteered. There's nothing like being with a herd of teen-agers to give one a new perspective on life." His smile was engaging.

"I'm sorry I don't have another cup of this life-giving liquid. Perhaps the foreman knows where we can find one. We could check," she suggested.

They walked over to the vortex of activity, where their request for another cup was quickly filled.

"Didn't I tell you Mike was efficient?" she asked. "A place for everything, and everything in its place." They sat down on the steps of the fellowship hall to watch the frenzied activities and drink their coffee. "I didn't know we were members of the same church," she said, her face slightly averted to ease the discomfort of his nearness.

"It's a big church," he said amiably. "Practically impossible to know everyone."

"Especially if you've been playing hooky as often as I have." She paused, her eyes straying up into the dawn-lit trees. "I've had a hard time coming here since Robert died. Inside, all I can see is the spot where Robert's body lay for the funeral service. To be honest, the only reason I'm here today is that I couldn't think of a graceful way to get out of it. Mike had laid his plans very carefully." She raised her hand in protest. "Please don't tell me I'll probably enjoy it once I get there. I know I will, but I just don't want to hear what I heard the whole time I was growing up."

Ethan's face crinkled, and he chuckled. "That was one of my father's favorite sayings, too. Sometimes I think the entire world is on instant replay."

"Here comes our fearless leader now. It must be time to head 'em up." The thought crossed her mind that Ethan would be a pleasant traveling companion, but things didn't work out for them to ride in the same van. She was strangely disappointed, then fussed mildly at herself for feeling that way.

They whizzed down the highway to the sound of happy singing with guitar accompaniment. "This reminds me of my college days," she told Mike as she rode beside him.

"Yeah, the music is one of the best parts of these outings." To prove his point, he began singing along with the group in a hearty baritone.

Beth didn't know the song and it made her feel a bit like an outsider, but the repeated chorus gave her a chance to join in part of the time. The contemporary hymn the young people were singing was filled with beautiful harmonies, but she felt the words were a little idealistic. Certainly they didn't fit in the real world as she knew it now, and for a moment she felt like a fraud. Obviously this was going to be a spiritual experience for all these people. For her, it would be only a pleasant change of pace. She had not given up her faith, but it had undergone enormous changes since Robert's death. *I guess the seeds are still there, but it's definitely wintertime for me*, she reflected.

The song ended and she took the opportunity to make conversation with Mike. "Why did you call me to be a chaperone? Did Pastor give you my name?"

"No, as a matter of fact, it was Dr. Stewart. He

said he had recently met you and felt you'd do a good job."

"Dr. Stewart?" So that's what Mike had meant when he said she was "what the doctor ordered." Or was he on a mission to save the lost and erring? The thought rankled.

She covered her annoyance by joining in as much as she could on the next song. But when they started singing the familiar words of the Twenty-third Psalm, she found herself in full rebellion. "I shall not want," they sang. *But I do want,* she thought, *I want Robert back. I want things the way they were. I want peace from my terrible dreams. I want my faith back.* An enormous lump formed in her throat, making it difficult to swallow the tears that threatened to spill from her dark eyes.

She thought the song would never end. When it finally did, she made no further attempts at light conversation with Mike, satisfied that he would not expect her to know the words to the newer youth songs.

Beth was glad when they finally pulled into the campsite, for the joyful praise had begun to wear on her nerves. But the crisp spring air brought back a degree of her usual cheerfulness.

The sun sifting through the trees dappled the ground like the coat of a spotted fawn. Nearby a river played over mossy-backed rocks, providing gurgling water music. Overhead, birds called to the forest creatures, warning of man's intrusion. It was too early in the year for the heat to have wilted the spring flowers, and they abounded in the clearing, spendthrift with their colors.

Ethan was in the middle of the tent-raising activities. She strolled over, carrying a box of cooking gear, determined to be civil to him. "Where do you want this stuff?"

"Here, let me help you," he offered.

26

"Are you *always* helpful?" she asked, with a bite of sarcasm in her voice.

He gave her a sidelong glance, sensing that all was not well in their new-found Garden of Eden, but he made no reply.

Taking the box, Ethan set it down in front of the newly secured tent. "Want to get a fire going?" he asked her, rubbing his hands together in happy anticipation. "We'll need lots of firewood for cooking and more for the evening campfire. I imagine it will get fairly cool tonight. I hope you brought enough warm clothes." His face radiated happiness.

"I've been camping before." She turned and walked to the edge of the clearing, hearing his footsteps behind her.

"Want to tell me what's wrong?" He picked up a piece of wood and waited patiently.

"Don't you ever go off duty?" she asked crossly.

"Not if I think I can help."

"Stop trying to help unless you're asked!" Her eyes were small thunderheads waiting for the lightning to develop. She jerked up a piece of wood and plopped it on the small stack cradled in her other arm. "Ethan Stewart, ever since I met you, I've been mad."

"Mother always said I was hard to get along with, and if I tried, I could probably be infuriating!" He gave her a crooked grin.

"Wipe that little-boy smile off your face; I'm immune to cuteness." She jerked up another piece of wood and pointed it at him with angry emphasis. "Did you think you'd get me out here in God's glorious woods and provide me with a religious experience earth-shaking enough to restore me to the fold?"

His arm shot out and slapped her hand, causing the log to crash to the ground. Coolly he said, "One of the first rules of camping is to watch where you put your hands." He ground the heel of his boot in the earth.

27

"There was a fiddleback spider heading for your hand."

Instantly all the wood she had gathered flew out of her arm, and she jumped back, awkwardly flailing her hands. "Ooooh," she shivered, "I despise *all* spiders regardless of their rank on the poison scale."

His eyes traveled the length of her jeans-clad figure. "I don't see any other dangerous creatures ready to devour you," he said. Noting her rosy cheeks, he added, "Is that high color anger or embarrassment?"

"You ask the dumbest questions," she shot back hotly.

"I like looking at you. You're very attractive."

Her blush deepened from rose to scarlet. "Thank you," she acknowledged lamely. "Are you always so frank?"

"God's beauties should be enjoyed *and* praised." He stooped down to retrieve the scattered logs. As she bent to help him, he captured her eyes with his. "I suggested to Mike that you would make an excellent counselor. But I mentioned it only because I thought you'd enjoy the outing. Nothing more." The honesty in his eyes was reassuring. "Still mad?"

"No." She lowered her feathery lashes. "Maybe you should treat me for paranoia."

"We'll save that for visit four," he said lightly. They rose together and started back to the campsite.

Remembering her brush with the deadly spider, she said, "I guess you're just a professional rescuer."

"Well, at least you're not still mad at me. I think we're making progress," he added cheerfully.

Her laughter floated through the tall pine branches.

The rest of the morning was spent in exploring the surrounding area and eating a quick picnic lunch. Beth was just putting the last crumbs of her potato chips away when one of the campers suggested a swim in a deep-pooled bend of the river. In minutes everyone was scrambling for swimsuits.

Beth adjusted the straps of her suit, suddenly aware that the top provided a revealing view. *What are you worrying about?* she chided herself. *You've worn this suit before.* She couldn't shake the wish that she were five pounds lighter, either. *Vanity, vanity. Couldn't be we're trying to impress the dear doctor, could it?* She grabbed up a towel and walked firmly out of the tent, determined to behave in her usual no-nonsense manner.

She spotted Ethan splashing around with some of the youngsters. When he saw her he climbed out of the water and came to meet her. Her heart did funny things in her chest as she watched him striding toward her, droplets of water cascading off his well-muscled chest.

"Coming in?" He ran his hand across his face and beard to wipe away the dripping water. "It's lovely."

She steeled herself for some comment on her appearance that didn't come. For a moment she couldn't decide if she were glad or disappointed.

"Is the water cold?" she asked.

"Not after you get in. Come on."

The sun glittered off the clear water, beckoning her. The cold water shocked her for only a moment, but she adjusted quickly. She paddled around, enjoying the caress of the tiny waves lapping at her body.

"I wonder why water is always so soothing?" she asked Ethan as they swam together.

"Remembrance of the womb, I suppose. It can be exhilarating, too." He deliberately smacked the water, splashing her face, and soon they were embroiled in a full-fledged fight that quickly spread to the entire group.

"King's X!" she cried as she dragged herself to the bank, panting from the exertion of the battle. She wiped her face dry and stretched out on the damp towel. "I feel like a kid again."

"That's what being with teen-agers can do for you," Ethan said as he plopped down beside her, and proceeded to shake his head like a shaggy terrier.

"Watch out! You're getting me all wet!" she cried.

"Isn't that statement a little redundant?" he asked as he cast his eyes over her very wet body.

"Touché," she said. Disdainfully she toweled off the water from her face and added, "I'm very impressed with your vocabulary."

"Just wait until you hear my doctor-talk. You'll be absolutely amazed." Still grinning, he stretched out full-length, his face turned toward the dancing sunlight.

Beth felt relatively safe in scrutinizing him as the sun forced his eyes shut. He wasn't remarkably handsome, but he was definitely pleasant to look at. Her eyes lingered on his lips.

They lay side by side in companionable silence. The sound of birdsong combined with the happy cries coming from the exuberant teen-agers at play was enough for the moment.

When Ethan turned over to sun his back, she broke the silence. "Do you work with the youth a lot?"

"Now and again. I play chaperone for them—or doctor—whenever they need one. I guess I'm in a dual role on this trip. Are you involved in any other church activities?"

She stiffened defensively. "Not now. After Robert died, the children needed me more than ever. I felt guilty about leaving them."

"Are you worried about them now?"

Her lips parted in surprise. "You know, I've barely given them a thought."

"Good. You deserve some time off. They're probably having a ball. Mrs. Reed will keep them so entertained they won't have time to miss you, either."

He propped his head up on his hand to look at her. "Tell me about your children."

"They're neat kids. I know I sound like the typical doting mother, but they're pretty cute. The other day Cally was playing with her glass of milk. I warned her to stop. Still she played with it. 'Are you deliberately trying to make a mess?' I asked her. 'No, I'm fixin' to have an accident'."

He laughed delightedly. "I love the logic of children." Soberly he added, "But it must be tough having full responsibility for them."

"Sometimes," she admitted. "The hardest part, though, is not having anyone to share those precious moments. I have only my mom and dad, and they live so far away." She turned over to face the friendly sun, closing her eyes against its brilliant rays.

"Is Cally in nursery school?"

She could feel his eyes on her face. It was a pleasant sensation. "Yes, but don't tell her. She thinks it's real school." Brows furrowed slightly, she slipped back into the recent past. "They're both in school now, but it was only yesterday that they were babies. I know they have only vague memories of Robert, and I feel so sad about that."

"My dad died when I was ten. There is a strange void when you grow up knowing your father only through old photographs."

"Thanks a lot for the reassurance," she said grimly.

"I was about to add," he continued, "that it was exciting also to discover pieces of him from other people. I love the larger-than-life picture I have of him. I may even know more about my dad than you do about yours." When she tried to protest, he held up a restraining hand. "Because I *worked* at it, and my information came from many sources, not just from a child's perspective."

"Maybe," she shrugged reluctantly. "Do you think

kids actually do benefit from being around other men—sort of father figures?''

"*You're* the expert." He sat up and surveyed the healthy young bodies still churning the water.

"It's one thing to know theory, but when it's your own children, you do a lot of questioning," she admitted.

"There's one sure way to cure all that. Take my advice and fall in love again. Isn't giving your children a father a good reason to be looking for a husband?"

"Ethan Stewart! That's the most cold-blooded thing I've ever heard!" She was sitting ramrod-straight, eyes registering indignation.

"Just practical, I'd say," he grinned at her.

She rejected his attempt at helpfulness and picked up her towel. "I really don't want to discuss this any more, and besides, it's time to start supper for this crowd." He made no effort to apologize which only angered her further. Without a backward glance, she strode to her tent to change into a pair of Levis.

There was no one in the six-person tent, and Beth sighed with relief: Ethan's words tumbled suggestively in her brain. Cold-blooded or not, he was probably giving her some good advice. *If* she fell in love again, it would be with someone who could love her children and be a good father to them. *Having kids certainly does complicate things*, she thought. And for a moment she knew a nostalgic longing for her young womanhood, days of courtship when the most pressing problem was getting a date with the latest man of her dreams. She grinned wryly to herself, knowing full well she wouldn't go back to those adolescent insecurities for anything. She was content to live in the present—problems, nightmares and all. She had learned too much to want to relive those experiences.

Throwing back the tentflap, Beth marched over to the cooking area. Mike was bent over the campfire, stirring a large pot. "Can I do anything to help?" she offered.

He wiped his smoke-filled eyes with the back of his hand. "Get me a gas mask, will you? I've moved all the way around this campfire, and the smoke gets in my eyes no matter where I stand!"

"They say smoke follows beauty," she chirped.

"Oh?" He looked up at her, red eyes streaming, soot on his cheek, and eyebrows in knots from squinting.

She couldn't help laughing and moved to lend a hand. "I suspect that this is not the best job in camp," she said, as she looked at the substance dripping off the oversized spoon. "What is this?"

"Campfire stew. It won't turn out right if it doesn't have a little sand and ashes mixed in," he grinned.

"I assume those ingredients have already been added." She didn't wait for an answer, but hurried on, eyeing the cauldron-sized container. "I'm not sure this spoon will reach to the bottom of this stuff—I mean stew. It seems to be getting a little thick down there."

"Here," said Ethan, striding up. "Let me do that." He took the spoon from her hand and gave the stew a masterful stir, then rearranged the smoldering logs to cut down on the cloud of smoke.

"Ever the expert, I see," was her caustic comment.

"I thought you said you'd been camping before," he teased, blue eyes shining with mirth.

"I have," she replied, a bit stiffly, "but we used a campstove."

"Not too practical for a group this size, I'd say."

And that group soon descended on them like the proverbial ravenous birds in the wilderness, stripping the gargantuan pot of its last particle.

It was just as the outdoor kitchen was being tidied and an impromptu game of tag beginning that the old bell mounted on a tall post clamored, calling everyone together for the evening devotions.

A towheaded youth and his sister softly strummed guitars as a tight circle of well-scrubbed teen-agers formed around the campfire.

Perhaps it was the soft voices that filled the night, or maybe it was the intense intimacy of the short devotional Mike gave; but whatever the reason, Beth felt more alone than ever. That loneliness swept away every other feeling, leaving no space for the special communion with God the others were sharing. As her eyes moved from the teen-agers' faces to Ethan's, her solitude became tinged with envy. *Why can't I feel His love for me? Where did it go?* She wanted to leave this worshipful circle. *I don't belong here.* Yet, the hope that something might jar loose the cold stone in her heart forged her more firmly into that circle.

Another contemporary hymn began and Beth desperately reached out for the words. A huge lump clogged her throat when she realized even the music failed to lift her. Mercifully Mike began to pray, giving her the excuse to close her eyes to the faces shining in the firelight.

As the campers quietly filed away, Beth followed, still empty. A single thought kept her moving. *I only have to stay one more day.*

CHAPTER 3

IT WAS IMPOSSIBLE to feel depressed the next morning when Beth awoke to the animated chatter of the girls.

From her bedroll, Beth surveyed the frenzied activity peculiar to bevies of preening females. All her tentmates were striving toward the common goal of becoming as attractive as the cosmetic industry could make them.

In the spirit of the day, Beth dressed quickly but carefully, hoping her turn at the campfire was over. In stark contrast to her fellow campers, she used her make-up lightly, knowing the heat and strenuous activities of the day would make quick work of a heavy-handed application. Peering into the tiny mirror propped up on her suitcase, she noticed her nose was a little sunburned. She smiled as she wondered if Dr. Stewart's was, too. And a feeling of anticipation accompanied her out of the tent at the thought of seeing him.

The heavenly aroma of bacon teased her appetite as she walked toward the campfire where Mike was skillfully handling a large iron skillet full of sizzling strips of browning bacon.

"Good morning, sleepyhead. You almost missed the best part of the day," he called as she approached. "I know, the first thing you want is a cup of hot coffee. There's hot water for instant."

"Great." She prepared herself a cup and surveyed the area over the rim as she took her first sip. "Where's Dr. Stewart?"

"He took a group on an early-morning hike. They should be back soon."

"I'm sure they will. They can probably smell that bacon all over the canyon."

Together they scrambled an unbelievable number of eggs and made camp toast over the grill. It was only minutes later that Ethan's shout sounded from the riverbank. He was followed by a frisky group of starved teen-agers who made short work of the plentiful breakfast.

"That's got to be the best food I've ever eaten in my whole life," Ethan breathed as he finished off his last cup of coffee.

"Find anything interesting out there this morning?" Beth walked over to the large tub being used to wash the dishes and dropped her cup in carefully, grateful that three sturdy boys were making a game out of the chore.

"Beauty, mostly. We hiked down the river a ways and then up the face of the wall. The best part of being on the top is looking down into the canyon. The river looks like a blue ribbon left out by a girl after a party."

"Why, Doctor, I had no idea you were so poetic. That was a lovely description."

"Thank you. And could we dispense with the 'doctor' stuff? Out here, it should be just Beth and Ethan. Time is too short to waste on titles and formality.

36

For one second Beth felt she might fall into those soft blue eyes and she covered her confusion by rushing on to another subject. "What time does the Bible study start?"

"In about ten minutes. We're going to have a short meeting all together, and then break into smaller groups for more intensive study."

"Oh. That should be interesting." It had been awhile since Beth had attended a formal Bible study and she wondered if she would be expected to be a leader. *They're only teen-agers*, she assured herself. *I can handle that*. "Is there a special passage or section we'll study together?"

"I think Mike intends to use the Twenty-third Psalm. The kids like the song that goes with it, and that ties everything together very neatly."

Inwardly Beth sighed with relief. *At least I know that one*.

The bell began its deep-throated clang and the crowd moved to the area where Mike stood under a giant cottonwood tree. He began his devotional with the reading of the psalm they all knew so well, but for Beth the words took on new meaning.

The top of the sheer bluff provided a "valley" for her to walk through with the psalmist. She didn't have to imagine the green grass and still waters; she could see them. *I know the Lord is my Shepherd. He has taken good care of all my physical needs, and I know I'll dwell in the house of the Lord forever. There's just that one part I haven't been able to reconcile yet.* The words kept running around and around in her head: "Thy rod and thy staff, they comfort me." *They haven't brought me comfort yet. Will they? When? I feel as though I know the beginning and the ending of the play, but the middle is still a blank.*

Beth knew the message of the psalm, the promise of God's never-ending love and care. It was used often as a song of comfort and assurance. That's what made it so painful in this time of spiritual drought.

Suddenly Beth heard her name called, and her five or six campers gathered on the sandy riverbank. It took a few minutes to settle down before Beth introduced the real reason for their time together.

"Well," said Beth, "how shall we begin?"

"You're the leader," countered a bright-eyed teen-ager.

"I'm not the sermon, though. This is *your* study. I'm only here to keep you from getting sidetracked."

"I don't really know exactly what this thing means," confessed one youngster. There was general agreement. "I know it says in picture language that the Lord takes care of us, but could we figure out exactly what it promises?"

"We can try." Beth read the first few verses from a traditional version of the Bible. "Do you have any idea what I just said?"

"I wish I knew," complained one. "Beats me," shrugged another. "Why does the Bible have to be so complicated anyway?" And it was this question that catapulted them into a daring new adventure. With rising enthusiasm the group recast the age-old poem in modern language, and when they had finished, Beth read back to them what they had composed.

The Lord is like a Super Dad, and takes care of everything I need. He gives me a good place to live and things to eat. He helps me when I'm in the worst kinds of trouble. He teaches me to lead a good life, for Jesus' sake. Even when I face death itself, I won't be afraid, because He is strong enough to keep me safe. He takes care of me and keeps me from being afraid. He made a banquet for me and in front of all the people who hate me, He crowned me and gave me the best of everything to eat. And He will keep doing this for me all my life, and when I die I'll live in heaven with the Lord forever and ever.

Silence followed the short reading. Beth noticed a look of dawning recognition on several faces. This was something each of them could understand—a direct promise from their Lord.

Beth hoped that none of the other adults would be offended by her attempt to help these young people understand what God was saying to them, but it really didn't matter what the others thought. Her kids had really dug in to learn, and she was proud of their work.

"Can we share this with the other kids?"

"Of course. I'm pleased that you want to." A loud whoop sounded, followed by general desertion of the group. *I guess we're through,* she grinned. One teenager ran back, shouting, "Thanks, Mrs. Martin. That's the best Bible study I've ever been to!" A heavenly warmth swept over her and a sense of gratitude for the challenge. She chuckled aloud as she realized that the Twenty-third Psalm would never be the same for her, either.

At that moment a piercing scream sounded throughout the canyon, echoing eerily. Beth was momentarily paralyzed, then started at a run in the direction of the cry. She could see a knot of campers leaning down over the rim of the canyon, reaching for a young girl who had obviously slipped over the edge. Her pulse racing crazily, Beth watched Mike and one of the boys pull the girl to safety. Several anxious minutes passed before they carried her to the campsite.

"What happened?" Beth queried Ethan.

"She just got a little too close to the edge. She'll be okay, I think. Mostly bruised, scratched, and scared, I suspect." His hands passed over the girl's limbs before he confirmed the diagnosis.

"Mike shouldn't have taken them so close to the rim," she said under her breath to Ethan.

"It was just an accident, Beth." He looked at her

calmly. "That's why I'm here—to help out at times like this."

"Still . . ."

"It was just an accident," he repeated. "She'll be fine, but Mike is feeling pretty bad right now. He doesn't need more punishment. Go pat him on the back or something. He needs more help than *she* does at this point."

But Beth was still angry at what she presumed to be Mike's carelessness and frightened anew when she visually measured the distance from the rim of the canyon to the floor. And though the girl hadn't actually fallen all that distance, she had had a close call. Beth spent her sympathy on the girl.

It didn't take the group long to recover from the incident and begin to make their plans for the next adventure. Roughly half of them wanted to follow the river to its source, a hardy climb amid tangled terrain; the other half chose to take the river's meandering course downstream.

Beth elected to go the easy route and was a little more than pleased when Ethan joined her. "Do you think they'll be all right?" she asked anxiously.

"Oh, I'm sure Mike will be able to handle things. You worry a lot, don't you?" They were wading in the cool water as the current gently washed over their tennis shoes.

A slight flush rose in Beth's cheeks. "I don't worry. I'm just very much aware of my responsibilities to this group."

"You're supposed to enjoy this outing, too. Perhaps you need a gentler hold on your responsibilities; you may be strangling them."

The glare with which she shafted him very nearly rivaled the sun. "I dislike people who promise to do something and then don't follow through. I'm not like those other people at the church."

Ethan took a cautious step forward in the river, and

40

in the conversation. "What did 'those other people' do to you?"

"It wasn't what they did; it was what they *didn't* do." She glanced up to check the position of the group and decided they weren't tuned in to the conversation. Turning, she confided to Ethan, "Today just reminded me that things never really change. After Robert's funeral everyone went back to the daily grind, and I was left with too many apple pies and no one to feed them to. One lady did call on me," she conceded, "but after that I was strictly on my own. They all said 'Call if you need anything,' but all I really needed was someone to talk with. Of course I didn't call. I knew they were busy with their own families."

"Is that why you didn't come back to church?"

"Partly. Mostly it was because I didn't fit any more. There are too many pairs, and I was a spare." A wan smile accompanied the statement.

"What about the organizations that have been formed for single people? Why didn't you join one of those?"

"I wasn't single." She bent over and picked up a small stone washed smooth by the water, held it, and examined it a trifle too long.

"Are you now?"

Caught off guard by the unexpected question, Beth's face revealed an utter lack of guile. "Why, I hadn't thought about it." An awkward silence developed as she pondered a question she hadn't considered in the two long years since Robert's death. "If you mean am I ready to get married again, I guess the answer is no. I'm still learning how to live by myself, how to take care of everything." She gave him just a tiny grin. "Living by myself does have some advantages. I'm not sure I'm ready for all the compromising that goes into the daily living with someone else. Robert and I had settled down very comfortably. We

41

both knew what was expected, who had which job."
This time the grin was wicked. "It takes a long time to
train a husband."

"Ooooh," he grimaced.

And in that instant, Beth noticed Ethan's mouth.
When a man's face is covered with a beard, she
thought, his mouth becomes a focus of attention,
looking vulnerable and unguarded. The impulsive
yearning to nestle in Ethan's arms, born in his office
the day he had listened to the first outpouring of her
grief, now gave way to the exquisite desire to kiss that
mouth and touch the beard. But she retreated from
those thoughts the moment she caught him watching
her.

Her embarrassment was acute. Hastily she began to
walk upstream, suddenly interested in what the others
were doing. Had he read her thoughts again? *Well, he
had started all this with his talk about marriage*, she
fumed silently. *I hadn't even thought remarriage until
he brought it up. And I'm definitely not going to give
him a chance to bring it up again.*

"Hey, it's not fair to shoot me down and then run
away. Give me a chance for rebuttal!" In trying to
catch up with her, Ethan stepped on a large flat stone.
Just as he shifted his weight, the stone tilted slightly,
forcing him into a spectacular balancing act with an
unhappy ending. "I missed!" was his cheerful com-
mentary as he sprawled in the shallow water.

Seeing that Ethan wasn't hurt, Beth laughingly
extended her hand to steady him as he rose to his feet.
Instead, he pulled her down beside him, making sure
she was as thoroughly soaked as he.

"That'll teach you to laugh at a helpless man!" he
said as they continued to splash each other.

Their spirit of joyous abandon was contagious, and
soon there wasn't a dry person in the bunch, as the
young people threw themselves into the mêlée. It was
a wet, but happy, gang that finally trudged into camp.

"I think I'll change into something a little less damp," said Beth as she headed for her tent.

"Nothing too fancy," Ethan called back. "Remember, it's your turn to cook!"

"Oh, brother, how could I have forgotten?"

The campfire was glowing evenly when Beth appeared, her hair toweled dry and curling in damp ringlets about her head. Thinking quickly, she unwrapped the packages of weiners, then suggested that each young person find a long stick and spear two or three weiners to be roasted over the fire. "Don't burn them!" she ordered, and continued setting out the buns, relishes and other condiments.

"Pretty smart, aren't you?" said Ethan as he accepted a plate.

"All teachers must undergo survival training," she shrugged aside the dubious compliment. "Besides, we need to use up all that unharnessed energy before starting home." She pointed in the direction of two young campers who were fencing with their hot dog sticks.

The sun was tipping over the back wall of the canyon before the last tent was folded and loaded into the van. It seemed natural for Beth to climb up beside Ethan. The gathering darkness and the dozing campers gave them another chance to talk, but Beth carefully steered the conversation away from herself.

"Why did you choose a family practice over a specialty?" she asked above the hum of the engine.

"I guess I thought I'd get tired of seeing nothing but bunions or backbones all day. I like the idea of knowing the entire family, of developing continuity. After I graduated from medical school, I came back home to take over my uncle's practice when he retired."

"Does your family still live here?"

"No, everyone has migrated south. I guess it's up to me to keep the family name alive in medicine here." He leaned his head against the back of the seat. "As my practice grows, I'll take in new doctors and expand into a family clinic." Even in the fading light she could see the glow of contentment on his face. "How about you? Do you aspire to be the superintendent of schools?" he asked, leaning forward to peer intently into her eyes.

"Oh, I don't think so. I'm happy where I am right now." But she wondered. Were there any goals left? Any dreams to give her life meaning and purpose? She was simply living the days one at a time. It was enough for now.

The road slipped by like a swift black river as they sped back to her life. The children would be waiting for her. A big smile floated dreamily across her face. In her children were invested all her dreams for tomorrow.

CHAPTER 4

I COULD RUN faster than this car is moving, Beth
fretted as she hurried to collect the children after the
two-day camp-out. Once she had pulled up in front of
Mrs. Reed's house, it seemed to take forever to get
out of the car and onto the porch, and another eternity
before the front door was opened.

"Hello!" said the grandmotherly little lady.
"We've been looking for you." Her words were
almost drowned out by the children's noisy greetings.

Beth barely made it inside the door to kneel down
and hug Sean and Cally simultaneously.

Their converstations ran together as they tried to fill
her in on their activities. " . . . and we made cookies
. . . shopping . . . got to watch a circus on TV. . . ."

"Whoa, one at a time. First, do you have everything ready to go? It's late and we need to get home."
As the children scampered to get their suitcases, she
turned to Mrs. Reed. "How can I ever thank you for
taking such good care of them?"

The petite woman's eyes misted slightly. "Thank

you for sharing them with me. I miss not having grandchildren. But that's another story.''

"Ah, Mrs. Reed, I think you and I may be able to work out a mutually satisfactory agreement,'' Beth smiled.

"Just call me Granny. Everyone does.'' Her face shone with pleasure "I've been a grandmother to at least half the children in this town.''

"Lucky children!'' said Beth sincerely.

The flurry of goodbyes took on a decidedly cheerful air, and they were on their way to their own home.

"Did you see any bears?'' asked a yawning Sean.

"No. I guess they'd all been captured, but we did play in a lovely river.''

"Did you at least get to sleep in a tent and cook out over a fire?'' Sean persisted.

"Yes, darling, and it's not nearly as much fun as you might think to cook for that many people.''

"Do we have to go to school tomorrow? Couldn't we just talk about all the things you did and all the things Granny let us do?'' Cally asked. "We have so much to talk about.''

"Yes to both questions.''

There was mild grumbling, but no mutiny as she tucked them into their little beds at last.

"A real bed,'' Beth murmured as she finally dropped, exhausted, into her own. "And a real stove to cook on in the morning.''

Beth's eyes drifted open slowly and focused on the clock beside her bed. Five-thirty. Not yet time to get up. But she felt so rested that she used the extra moments to relive parts of the camping trip, specifically the parts with Ethan Stewart. He had raised some interesting questions, and aroused some long-buried feelings.

She fought the vivid image of her husband lying beside her. Sleeping, he had always looked so utterly defenseless, so vulnerable, and she had often reached out to touch an errant curl as it fell over his forehead. And those mornings when he awakened and reached for her . . . *No, no, don't think! Don't remember!* she commanded her heart. Besides, theirs wasn't always a fairy tale romance.

Bittersweet came the memory of their first fight over an expensive dress she had longed to wear to an important party. She had asserted her will and bought the dress against Robert's expressed wishes. *Surely,* she remembered thinking, *when he sees me, he'll recant.* But Beth was unprepared for Robert's total anger when she twirled expectantly into the room that night, modeling the gown for his approval. In the end she had worn it to the party, but it would never be a happy dress and it had hung in the back of her closet for a long time before she finally gave it away.

Now there was no one to fight with over budgets or vacations . . . no one for early-morning cuddlings or nights of love. She still preferred to recall their marriage without the voices raised in anger, the icy silences, for there had been so many more good and joyous times.

Beth roused herself as the alarm went off and walked to the bathroom for her shower, acutely aware that there was not one masculine item in sight. Slowly she slid one of the drawers open and took out a small bottle of shaving lotion. It was one of the few things of Robert's she had kept. She opened the bottle and breathed deeply of its spicy fragrance. With her eyes closed, she could almost feel his presence in the room . . . toweling off after his shower . . . drawing her to him for a quick morning kiss . . .

"Mom."

The bottle dropped from her hand and splattered against the sink. "Oh, Sean, you scared me, son!" Picking up the pieces of glass, she composed herself quickly.

"I'm sorry, Mom! I heard you in here and I wanted to ask if I could make the orange juice this morning."

"It's okay. I just didn't hear you come in. Yes, you can make the juice." She felt helpless anger rise at the loss of the precious bottle, but Sean had meant no harm. She could replace the shaving lotion. It just wouldn't be Robert's.

Sean was watching her with solemn eyes. "Was that Dad's shaving lotion?"

"Yes."

"It smells like he's in here." Tears brimmed in his eyes.

"I know." She knelt down and put her arms around her small son. "Sometimes when I'm lonely for your dad, I open the bottle and it makes me feel closer to him." A tear slid down Sean's cheek at the sight of the glass shards. "It's all right. I can buy another one, Sean. It will still smell the same. But right now I need to get the glass picked up. You can help me best by getting Cally up and making that juice. Okay?"

"Okay." Sean didn't scamper out the door as he usually did. There was a purposeful stride that hadn't been there before.

Beth hated to wash out the sink, but she was afraid of leaving any slivers of glass, so she washed the rest of the lotion away, too.

Putting away the past, she showered quickly. As she thought about the day ahead, she realized with a start she hadn't had a bad dream in almost a week. Maybe all she had needed was the reassurance of the doctor to relieve her mind. And the camping trip had certainly been refreshing. Things were beginning to look up.

Her day at school went well, or maybe it was knowing that there were only two more weeks left in the year. At odd moments she speculated about what she and the children would do with the lovely first week of their glorious free time, but the phone cut short her train of thought.

"Hello? Oh, hello, Ethan." The deep timbre of his voice caught her totally off guard, and she sank back into her chair, slightly weak.

"I just called to see if you had recovered from the campout."

"Recovered, and grateful for my own bed," she laughed.

"Maybe you wouldn't say no to another camping trip later in the summer."

"Maybe I wouldn't," she agreed.

"Actually, I called for another reason, too."

A prickle of anticipation stirred. "Yes?"

"There's a singles' party at the church next Friday night and I'd like for you to go with me. Would you?"

Mild shock was her first reaction. No one had asked her out in all this time. "Well . . . I don't know."

"Would you check that busy calendar of yours and see if the evening is free? I think you'd enjoy the party. We're going out for pizza and then to see a movie."

His low-key approach was not at all threatening. It would have been easy to refuse, but having spent time recently with other people, Beth was newly aware that she had missed socializing. *What harm could there be in a movie?* she rationalized. *Ethan was a nice man.*

"What time?"

His smile was apparent even over the phone. "I'll pick you up about six. Okay?"

"Okay." Her spirits lifted at the thought of being with other adults, but there was no denying that it was Ethan whose presence she preferred. She replaced the receiver and reached for the little red book listing names and numbers of friends. *I'll need to call Granny to keep the kids while I'm out,* she thought. She couldn't quite bring herself to call this a date.

But Cally wasn't as reticent about euphemisms. "Where are you going on your date?" she questioned, watching her mother carefully as Beth stood at the closet door, trying to decide what to wear.

"It's not really a date, Cally. Dr. Stewart and I are just going to eat pizza and see a movie with a lot of other people from the church." *The burgundy sweater with matching slacks? Hmmm.*

"Well, what would you be doing if it was a 'really' date?" she persisted logically.

"Go out to dinner, I suppose." *Maybe the yellow dress.*

"Well, you won't be hungry when you get through eating pizza, will you, Mommy?"

"Oh, Cally," Beth replied irritably, "will you stop the questions? Okay, let's call this a 'really' date."

"Does that mean you don't love Daddy any more?" Her brown eyes were forlorn.

There it was. The real question Cally had been wanting to ask. The one Beth didn't want to hear. She walked over to the bed where Cally waited for her answer. Putting her arms around the child, she pulled her close. "I still love your daddy, honey, but I need to spend some time with other grown-ups. This isn't going to change anything in our lives." She kissed the soft forehead and nuzzled the light brown hair. "Is Sean worried, too?"

"He says he's not, 'cause he loves you harder than Dr. Stewart does."

"And I know I love you both harder and harder every day! Besides, I doubt very seriously if Dr. Stewart loves me at all. We're just becoming friends."

"That's what Sissy's mother says everytime she gets a new boyfriend," sighed Cally. "I guess we're just like everybody else now." There seemed to be some perverse comfort in that thought.

Beth felt a sinking sensation in the pit of her stomach. Despite her glib reassurances to Cally,

50

things would *not* be quite the same once she took her first tenuous step out of widowhood.

I didn't ask for this life! Beth fumed. *Certainly didn't plan for it.* With a simple "okay" she had been forced to acknowledge her singleness. Married, but not married. She hated all the national attention that was focused on what had come to be called the "swinging singles" lifestyle. She knew her life would never take that direction, but going out with Ethan, no matter what she called it, was not the act of a married woman. "This had better be one terrific movie!" she murmured to herself as she put on the burgundy slack set.

"I'll get it!" shouted Sean at the sound of the doorbell.

Granny Reed was warmly welcomed and quickly given a tour of each child's room where she exclaimed over treasures shared with her.

The doorbell rang again, this time signaling Ethan's arrival. A quiver of excitement swept over Beth as she let him into the house. Just seeing him brought heightened color to her cheeks and took her breath. It was a peculiar sensation, one she hadn't experienced since her teen-age years. It also made her feel a little silly. *He's only my doctor*, she reminded herself. *Just a friend*.

Brief introductions were made and the children returned to their activities with Granny, even more eager to be with her than with their mother's new friend.

Quickly Beth and Ethan were on their way, and Beth was relieved that none of the negative feelings expressed earlier had spilled over. It was a clean getaway.

Beth could not suppress a feeling of guilt, for her instincts told her she was doing something she shouldn't. Yet, as they made their way carefully through the first awkward moments together, she began to relax. She was amazed at how young Ethan seemed, even more amazed when she remembered he was several years older than she. *But I feel so much older*, she thought ruefully. *It is true, I suppose. Children do age you.*

Being with Ethan was pleasant. There were no conversational gaps, for others filled in whenever there was a moment of silence during the meal. Beth felt immediately at ease with the group. It was apparent they met frequently and enjoyed one another immensely.

Later, at the movie, Beth became absorbed at once, even laughing at some of the humorous dialogue. But, when a love scene began, she shifted uncomfortably. With a start she realized the male lead reminded her of the man sitting next to her—maybe it was the beard. But she blushed when the hero kissed the heroine passionately. Unaccountably she could feel the intensity of that screen kiss on her own lips, and with a stirring she thought long buried. There was genuine relief when the scene ended, and the comedic story line resumed.

Afterward, their goodbyes were friendly and brief, each declaring the success of the evening. And then Ethan was gone and Beth was safely back in her own house, surprised it had all ended so quickly. She wasn't sure she had planned to have a good time, but she had. A small feeling of victory glowed within her, as if she had passed some sort of test.

"Thank you again, Granny," Beth said as she saw her out the door.

"Any time. But I would like to spend some time with you, too, my dear. Such wonderful children must have a wonderful mother." She beamed and added, "Why don't you three come over for Sunday dinner? I'd just love to cook for a family again."

"Why, that would be lovely. May I bring something?"

"Absolutely not. See you around twelve-thirty Sunday—after church," Granny called back over her shoulder.

The table had been laid with a snowy cloth and Granny's best china and silverware. Heavenly smells wafted from the kitchen, and, with Beth's help, Sean and Cally helped put the serving bowls on the table.

"We're almost ready," declared a rosy-faced Granny. "That is, we're ready—as soon as the other guest arrives."

The words were barely out of her mouth when the doorbell rang.

"Ah," was all Granny said and hurried to the door.

Beth stood with her lips parted in surprise as Ethan Stewart stepped into the room.

"Hello, Ethan," Granny smiled beatifically, her white updo haloing her face.

Mutual laughter bubbled between Ethan and Beth.

"Hello, Beth, I'm glad to see you again," said Ethan cheerfully. "Hello, Sean and Cally. Granny's been telling me a lot of nice things about you two." He gave Beth a penetrating look. "I already know a lot of nice things about *you*." From behind his back he produced a large bouquet of spring flowers. "And these are for my best girl," he said, giving Granny a big kiss on the cheek.

"Oh, Ethan, you're always so thoughtful! Let me just get these in some water while you take your places at the table. Ethan, your usual spot, and the rest wherever you like. How lovely to have a family to cook for!" and she scurried into the kitchen to find a vase.

Ethan pulled out a chair for Beth and helped the children find their seats. "I love Granny's Sunday dinners. It reminds me so much of home." It seemed to Beth that he was completely at ease—he must come here often. "I can tell by the look on your face that you weren't expecting anyone else," he said, taking his own place at the head of the table. "Just relax and let Granny enjoy her surprise," he whispered.

She bustled back into the room and seated herself beside Beth. "Ethan?" she asked and bowed her head.

"Lord, we thank You for all Your bounty and the friends around our table. Amen."

"Amen," they echoed.

"And what culinary delights have you prepared today, Granny?" Ethan asked, unfolding his napkin.

She uncovered the main dish with a flourish. "Rock cornish hens stuffed with your favorite dressing."

As one of the small birds was placed on Sean's plate, he asked in a stage whisper, "Are these baby chickens, Mom? I don't think I can eat a baby chicken."

Amid the gentle laughter, explanations were made and he was delighted with the tiny drumstick cut for him. "Billy won't believe me when I tell him I ate a whole chicken by myself, will he, Mom? You'll have to tell him it's true."

Beth noticed Cally's unusual silence, but it wasn't until the end of the meal, over German chocolate cake, that she finally spoke.

"Granny, can we do this next week, too?"

"Well, goodness gracious, I guess that's about the best compliment a cook could receive, Cally dear! Of course, we can do it again—as often as you want to. Except that next Sunday I already have a dinner invitation. But let's try for the week after that, shall we?"

When it came time to clean up, everyone pitched in and finished the chore in short order. As the last of the dishes was put away, Granny said, "You big guys will have to entertain yourselves. Sean and Cally and I are going to play some serious 'Go Fish'," and with that she rummaged around in the drawer of the old mirrored buffet for a deck of cards.

"Want to walk off part of that feast?" Ethan asked Beth.

"Sounds good."

They strolled into Granny's carefully manicured back yard, where roses were spilling their fragrant perfume into the late afternoon air. Overhead, in the trees delicately laced with new growth, the birds seemed destined to burst their lungs in an effort to match the beauty of the flowers.

"I hope you aren't angry with Granny. Matchmaking is one of her hobbies," Ethan said as they sat under a shade tree in an old garden swing.

"I could never be angry with someone who makes all of us so happy. I should think, though, that you'd be the uncomfortable one."

"Not with Granny. She likes me and she likes all of you. What could more natural than wanting good friends to be together?"

"I gather you've known each other for quite awhile." Beth's eyes drifted over the neatly kept geranium beds.

"She almost married my uncle when they were both young, so she still considers me family. He was the bachelor doctor in town and she was one of the town beauties. But in one of those silly quirks of fate, she married someone else, and so did he. They have remained friends all these years. Still write, I suspect. The four of them spent a lot of time together before Granny's husband died about five years ago. After that, my uncle and his wife moved, so she was pleased to have another bachelor to fuss over. And here I am, loving every minute of it."

"So are the children." The swing glided slowly back and forth. "They've needed a grandmother to do the things parents can't. Granny more than fills that bill. It's nice to have the feeling of family."

"Speaking of family, are you planning to see your parents when school is out?"

"Oh, yes, the children can't wait to visit their grandparents. And I have to attend several workshops." Beth realized, with surprise, that she was actually enjoying the small talk—nothing pressing, no decisions to make. "But the thing I'm most looking forward to," she confessed, "is the chance to do nothing but spend time with my children. If I didn't have my summers, I'd never be able to make it through the school year."

He nodded with understanding. "Working with children all day can be emotionally exhausting—not to mention the responsibility you have at home. But burnout occurs in the medical profession, too. I make a point of taking time off from the routine—doing things that have nothing to do with medicine."

"Like chaperoning campouts?" she smiled.

"Yes. I like working with the elderly, too." Ethan leaned back comfortably, stretching out his legs. "Elderly people are fascinating. They've experienced so much. It's a shame that in this country there's no honor in living a long time. Why, they're walking history books!" he sat erect, growing enthusiastic with the sharing of his discovery. "Granny and I are working on a local project. We're asking some of the oldtimers to tape their recollections for the library. It will give the public an informal oral history of this area."

Beth's interest piqued and she turned to face him. "You are a man of surprises, aren't you?" She found herself studying Ethan's face with a new awareness. She still knew very little about him, in spite of the time they had spent together.

"Granny was the one who inspired the project.

She's full of stories about the old days. It was her idea to tape some of them."

"Do you mountain climb and fight bulls, too?" she teased.

"No, but I travel occasionally, and I dabble in photography. Portraits, mostly. I have some good studies of the people who have taped their oral histories. I felt their faces as well as their stories should be recorded for posterity." The sun's rays struck his beard, and sparks of gold glinted among the rust. "We could use some help this summer, if you're interested. Granny needs someone to go with her when she makes her jaunts into the country. I don't like for her to be alone, and I'm not always free to go with her."

A vague sense of disappointment flitted through Beth at the thought that Ethan would not be accompanying them, but she responded gamely, "I'd love to help out," and added, "I'm sure the children would, too."

"Mom!" called a small voice from the back porch. "Granny says we can make ice cream. Okay?" Sean sprinted down to them. "She said Dr. Stewart would have to turn the dasher, though. What's a dasher?"

"I rest my case," laughed Beth.

"Come on, Sean, let me introduce you to one of the true pleasures of life—licking the dasher."

It was a golden day, one of those rare treasures one stashes away and takes out from time to time for savoring. The picture of Granny putting the rich cream mixture into the old-fashioned churn for Ethan to turn; Sean's manly try as it thickened; Cally, sitting on Ethan's lap, feeding him quick melting bites of the icy delight. Seeing the man's kindness to her children in a home filled with Granny's love brought quick tears to Beth's eyes. But what made the tears spill over was the thought that the man should be Robert. It just wasn't fair! No matter how kind Ethan was, he

57

was not Cally and Sean's father. Robert was irrevocably gone from them.

"More ice cream?" Ethan spoke close to her ear.

On the pretext of putting her dish in the sink, she turned away to hide her tears. In control again, she managed a too-bright smile. "No, thanks. I couldn't eat another bite."

Ethan had read her heart, for she saw compassion registered in his eyes, heard it in his voice. "Sadness on such a happy day?"

"I'm fine, Doctor. Just a touch of nostalgia." Suddenly she felt very tired. "I hate to be a party-pooper but tomorrow is a schoolday for some and a working day for others." She anticipated the groans of protest and dealt with them swiftly. Within a reasonable length of time, there were goodbye hugs and promises of more good times.

"Good night, Ethan. We all had a lovely time," she said formally, when they were at last ready for home.

"I think I enjoyed it almost as much as the children," he responded. "Good night, Sean and Cally," and he gave each of them a bear hug.

Ethan left Granny's house as Beth and the children did. His car followed hers for a block or so before turning off, and then they were alone in the night on the way back to their own home. A gentle joy sustained Beth at the thought that she would not be going home to an empty house. She had taken two of the reasons for the happiness of the day home with her. And it didn't take her long to get them tucked into bed.

The house was secure for the night as Beth went to her own bedroom to get ready for bed and some late-night reading. Reaching for the light switch to her bathroom, she froze. She could swear someone was in the small room, or had just been there before her. The faint smell of aftershave assailed her senses. Robert's aftershave. With herculean effort Beth flipped the

58

switch, flooding the room with light. No one was in sight.

Of course there's no one here! she scolded herself. *Some of the lotion must have splashed on the carpet when I dropped the bottle.*

She had intended to take a warm bath and read herself to sleep, but she was so shaken that she simply turned off the bathroom light, shut the door and dropped onto her bed.

I'll just read for a while, she thought. Slipping off her shoes, she propped herself up on the pillows and blindly turned a few pages of the book. Her eyes kept straying off the page to the closed door. *He's not here*, she reminded herself. *Robert is dead and will never be in this room again. He's dead!* She tried logic. *You're feeling guilty because you have spent some pleasant times with Ethan Stewart, and the shaving lotion just served as a reminder of Robert. Did you expect to find an irate husband lurking in the shadows? You've done nothing wrong. Remember that. Nothing.*

Resolutely, she picked up her book. But she couldn't concentrate, and her eyes began to droop as she drifted off into a troubled sleep.

And the dream came again. This time when she entered the cold stone building, she noticed that it had some type of fancy windows. She recognized them, though their true significance remained just beyond her comprehension.

The man was waiting on an elevated platform at the far end of the huge room. It seemed to take forever to walk the length of it. As she approached, her heart constricting within her chest, the floor rose before her, forming steps that would take her to that dreaded balcony. She knew the fire would soon be visible, reaching out for her with greedy tongues. Waiting for the searing pain that was sure to accompany the flames, she woke with a silent scream locked in her throat.

For a moment Beth was paralyzed with fear and drenched with perspiration from her brush with death. Then she lunged from her bed. It was imperative that she talk with someone. She reached for the phone, but whom was she calling? She slammed down the receiver and paced the room, trying to shake the fog of her dream.

Picking up the phone again, Beth decided to call Ethan. He was the only one who really knew about the dreams. Fumbling, she cradled the receiver against her shoulder while she thumbed through the "S's" in the directory. She could not bring herself to surrender the phone—her safety line—even for a moment. Suddenly Ethan's face floated comfortingly before her. Ethan, laughing, as Cally fed him ice cream.

Slowly she hung up. As she focused on reality, her panic diminished. But Ethan was more than her doctor now. She had spent too much time with him socially to think of him in a strictly professional manner. Perhaps he would think it odd if she called him in the middle of the night just after spending the day together.

Beth drew a deep breath, and her head began to clear. It was only a bad dream—and not the first. She had made it through the ordeal without Ethan before; she could do it again.

Walking to the bathroom Beth opened the door and turned on the shower. Stripping off the clothes she had not changed before falling asleep, Beth stepped under the warm spray. The fragrant soap lathering her body floated away the residual fear. The hot spray pulsating against her skin relaxed tense muscles, and the fluffy towel soothed ragged nerves. Slipping a cotton gown over her head, she padded to the kitchen for a cup of warm milk.

Returning to the bedroom, she sprinkled talcum powder over the pillows and climbed into her bed, breathing a prayer for peace. A sense of tranquility crept over her, bringing much-needed rest. Why did she so often forget to pray until a crisis? And knowing Ethan was available also helped to foster the courage to fight her lonely battle. It wasn't necessary to tell him she had wanted to call him. Besides, she had no special claim on his time. Busy doctors needed their sleep, too.

"Mom! Get up! It's almost time to leave for school!" The sound of Sean's urgent voice propelled Beth out of bed, and her anger in starting the day at a dead run fueled her flight.

"I hate Mondays!" she muttered under her breath as she fought the morning traffic. She really didn't expect the day to get any better. And it didn't.

Outside her office sat the same children, waiting for a scolding. It annoyed her that she was unable to help them change their behavior. *The same kids; the same speech!*" she fumed.

She picked up her buzzing phone.

"Mrs. Watkins. Line one."

And the same mothers. Beth was careful to unclench her teeth before she said, "Hello, this is Mrs. Martin."

By the time she had managed to dismiss the tiresome woman, Beth was sure she was caught up in another of her nightmares.

That night, when they were all assembled at home, Beth relied on a simple menu for supper—a fluffy omelet and biscuits, with some of Granny's preserves. She was too tired for anything more elaborate, and her head ached from her interrupted sleep and the rigors of her day.

"I wanted pizza," complained Sean.

"Me, too," fussed Cally.

"I'm not going to go out and buy pizza when I have a perfectly good supper half-cooked," she stated flatly.

It was a dismal meal, filled with discontent. The children continued to let her know how unhappy they were with her lack of cooperation by quarreling over the slightest things.

Bedtime couldn't come too early for Beth, but the evening sun still hung onto the day, refusing to give her an excuse to hurry them to bed.

"But it's still daytime!" Sean and Cally chorused.

As she tucked them in for the third time, she thought, *At least I can wake up from a nightmare.*

CHAPTER 4

SCHOOL'S OUT. sighed Beth.

The children had already done their time for the year. Now it was her turn. Everything was neatly filed away and ready for the coming fall. Except for the custodians, the building was empty when Beth locked her office for the last time.

The rhythms of her life had risen and fallen to the cycle of the school year since she was five years old, and the familiar feelings of the last day of school swept over her. Ahead were lazy days and activities—mostly of her own choosing.

Her heels tapped out a goodbye message that echoed up the empty halls and, as she hurried home, a half-guilty feeling of forbidden freedom spurred her on.

The days were hot now, and the trees heavy with foliage. Even with the air conditioning on, Beth knew the heat outside was waiting for an opportunity to encase her in its humid arms. Pulling onto her street, she saw her children languidly tossing a ball back and forth.

"They look so limp," she said to herself, "and the summer has just begun. I wonder where I put that sprinkler toy."

Sean frowned when she suggested that they play in the cool water in the front yard. "Why can't we go next door and swim instead," he complained.

"Because I don't see the flag. You know that if the flag isn't up, you're not invited over. That's been the arrangement since they got the pool. Play for a while and I'll call you for a nice cool supper."

Sean turned his back, but she clearly heard him mutter, "Some way to start the summer. Baby stuff."

Swiftly she caught up with him and knelt down to his level. "Hey, I just got home. I'm sorry if you're ready for a full-fledged vacation, and I'm not. I want this to be a good summer for all of us, but I don't want to start it right this minute." It suddenly occurred to her that she had to look up to see into Sean's eyes. "I just realized how much you've grown this winter. You're going to be a second-grader!"

He smiled widely, revealing a missing front tooth. "Yes," he lisped. "I hope I get Mrs. Pēna next year."

"Tell you what. Maybe it's time for a big guy to learn to swim. Shall I set you and Cally up for swimming lessons?"

"Yeah! But do they teach little kids?" He pointed to his smaller sister.

"Well," she whispered, "not quite as well as they do you big guys." And they shared a conspiratorial wink. "I'll call tomorrow and find out all the information." Sean's empty-spaced smile was reward enough.

All day Saturday, the day she should have felt totally relaxed, something was nagging at Beth. Was it something she had left undone? She checked the calendar by the phone to see if there was something planned for the upcoming week. *Tomorrow is Sunday,* she thought and wrinkled her brow in concentration. The square was blank. Above it was the small notation: "Dinner with Granny." *Ethan Stewart*, her mind flashed, and a tiny tingle teased her neck. Then she recalled Granny's previous commitment. There wouldn't be a golden Sunday afternoon this week.

A vague void flitted over the week to come. There was not a single mark on the entire calendar. The time was hers to spend as she chose. *Maybe I ought to take the children to church. We all need to get back into the Sunday routine*, she thought guiltily. Disquiet and commitment tugged at her. *It's been a long time*.

Memories of happy days fluttered through her mind like the pages of an old photo album. Everyone, clean and neat, hurrying to sit in the usual pew. Quick lunches. Putting the small children down for afternoon naps so she and Robert could spend special time together. Lazy afternoons at the lake. Their family life had been so—so normal.

The sudden hunger for all those dear days doubled her over with an almost physical pain, and she clutched her stomach. Tears sprang to her eyes. *It isn't fair! It just isn't fair!* she raged silently. Reaching for a small piece of those memories, Beth made a decision to take the children to church. *Just once*, she reasoned. Maybe there would be a crumb of happiness on her plate of despair.

It was a pleasant chore to lay out clean clothes for Sean and Cally that night. Shoes were polished and small heads shampooed.

Sean had only one question. "Do I have to wear a suit and tie?'

"No, darling. Just a nice shirt and pants."

Cally was quick to choose her blue dress. "'Cause I can button it by myself. I think Dr. Stewart will like it, too. He goes to church every Sunday. He told me so. Are we going to go every Sunday, too?" Cally crawled under the colorful sheet and snuggled against her pillow.

"I think it's time, don't you?" Beth asked serenely.

"Good. Then we can see him every single Sunday. Do you think it would be all right if I sit with him?"

An amused smile flirted with Beth's mouth. "I think we'd better sit together as a family this first time. Dr. Stewart may already have someone to sit with him."

Cally thought about this problem for a second. "Couldn't he share?"

"Yes, my dearest, but tomorrow may not be the best time to ask that of him. Why don't we just plan to be together for our first day back? Good night. Sleep tight."

It was good to see some of the familiar faces, but Beth was also aware that during her absence many, many new ones had been added to the fast-growing church family. Mike's greeting was enthusiastic, and she was genuinely glad to see him again. She didn't see the face she was looking for, though. And she knew Cally was disappointed, too.

But disappointment was only one of the many feelings she experienced that morning. To her chagrin, a well-meaning lady welcomed her and asked Beth to sign the visitor's roll. *It has been a long time.*

Granny welcomed them with open arms and gathered them to herself like a mother hen, shooing them into the pew with her.

The children were reasonably well-behaved, leaving Beth plenty of time to listen to the sermon.

It was the Sunday dedicated to Pentecost, when the Holy Spirit had come to the multitude in the form of tongues of fire—a time of rededication traditionally observed in the Christian church. The strong sermon hit a nerve on more than one occasion for Beth. One biblical quote in particular kept echoing in her mind,

66

sending her off on a silent theological argument with God. "I have called you by name and you are Mine."

It offended her logic to think God could love her so much, yet take Robert . . . or at least allow him to die. What kind of God would do that? All the esoteric debates she had ever had with nonbelievers about the existence of God returned to haunt her.

God, if You have chosen me, give me some kind of sign, she prayed silently. *Show me in some way that You still love me.*

There was no sudden bolt of lightning. The earth didn't quake or even quiver. The cross over the altar remained firmly attached to the wall. The stained-glass windows depicting the crucifixion did not spring to life. But her eyes continued to sweep the church in search of something extraordinary.

The small sigh of disappointment that escaped Beth caught Cally's attention, and the child snuggled up closer, smiling contentedly. It had not been so the last time she had cuddled up to Beth in church, for that had been a sorrowful day. But try as Beth might, she could not recapture the scene in her mind's eye.

There was no death here. It was a joyful day filled for the most part with people she didn't know—not friends and relatives with long faces. It was with a deep sense of relief that she realized that sad day was long ago in the past, a past that was fading with each new experience. *It's like growing up again, one step at a time,* she thought. She felt a smile parting her full mouth, and she gave Cally a loving squeeze. There was more than a crumb on her plate. God had given her a choice morsel, and she breathed a prayer of thanksgiving.

It was at that moment she spotted Ethan carrying offering plates up to the minister at the altar and her smile broadened. Was the Lord trying to tell her something?

After the final hymn was sung, there was a muted rumbling of after-church visiting in the pews.

"I wish all of you were coming home with me for lunch." Granny looked wistful. "But you will come next Sunday?" The little blue straw sailor hat atop her snowy pompadour bobbed up and down in delight with Beth's affirmative answer.

"Of course, Granny. You have a lovely time today and we'll all get together next Sunday."

As they moved with the flow of human traffic out the massive doors, Beth casually scanned the faces for a glimpse of Ethan. He caught her eye and began to work his way through the crowd. A gentle rush of pleasure trickled over her as he sought her out.

"Good morning! I'm glad to see you!"

Ethan's surprise at her presence irked Beth momentarily, but her irritation passed as he patted each child affectionately. "Good morning, yourself," she greeted him. "You look chipper today."

"And you look lovely. I like that dress."

Beth smiled at the compliment, glad she had worn her favorite frock with its soft drapes that accentuated her best features. The neckline was modest, but gave a subtle hint of the lush curves hidden there.

"Granny stood me up for lunch. What are you going to do?"

She shrugged her shoulders. "We haven't made any plans. Snack, I suppose."

Ethan looked at the fidgety children beside her, bored with adult conversation and eager to be off. "How would you two like some hamburgers followed by a boatride on the lake? Okay, Mom?" he asked over their enthusiastic yeses.

"How could I possibly say no?" she laughed.

"Okay! I know just the place." His eyes reflected the children's excitement.

Plans for the outing were swiftly made and efficiently executed. In a relatively short time the four

68

of them were skimming over the water, damp from the deliciously cool spray thrown up by the speeding boat.

Sean was sitting in the front, Beth in the seat beside Ethan, and Cally behind them. Ethan steered the boat across the large lake, staying well clear of the other boats pulling water-skiers.

The summer sun warmed Beth's skin, relaxing tense muscles and providing soul-satisfying peace. The calmness of the water was churned up by several boats, changing the deep blue water a frothy aquamarine.

Ethan headed for a quiet cove and idled the motor, letting the children take turns guiding the boat.

Beth turned to the smiling man beside her. "You know just how to make them happy. Why haven't you married and had your own?"

"Oh, I almost did, several times." His smile was self-deprecating.

The answer only teased her curiosity. "And . . ." she coaxed.

"It's a dull story of mismatches that fortunately failed just in time." His beard was beaded with droplets. Very white teeth emphasized his mobile and sensuous mouth as he smiled. "Right now, I just enjoy other people's children and then give them back when they're dirty or cross."

"Like my friend who loved to stir up the baby and the dog, and then go home."

"Guilty."

With Ethan behind the wheel again, they criss-crossed the lake, the sound of the motor and the camaraderie between them making conversation unnecessary.

At dusk they headed back to the dock, the retreating sunlight leaving behind shadowy footprints along the shore.

Ethan built a small fire and they roasted weiners in

69

the licking flames. The warm night filled with flickering stars and a full moon cast silvery light into every corner of their little camp.

"This reminds me of our camp-out," said Beth.

Cally's ears pricked up. "Is this what it's like to camp out?"

"Sort of—except we slept in tents." And before the children could get any ideas, she quickly added, "But we don't have a tent to sleep in tonight."

An owl hooted in the quiet night, adding his soft call to the sound of the waves lapping gently at the shore.

"I don't think I'm ready to sleep outside yet, Mom," Cally shivered.

Ethan put his arms around Cally. "That's just an old hoot owl. He's probably calling to his girl friend."

Cally giggled. "Owls don't have girl friends, do they?"

"Sure they do. Where do you think all those little owls come from?" Ethan teased.

"From eggs."

"Touché." Ethan smiled at the puzzled look on Cally's face. "That means, 'You win.'"

Cally nodded her head, looking wiser.

Watching the firelight play across the planes of Ethan's face, Beth was again struck by the kindness she saw illuminated there. That breathtaking moment in his office when she had felt the irresistible urge to nestle in his arms came sweeping back over her. Again, as he sat across the fire from her, she experienced a desire to touch him that was so strong she almost rose and walked over to him Only the children's presence prevented her carrying out her intention. She ducked her head in private embarrassment and forced her eyes to focus on the tiny dancing flames. "It's getting late," she mumbled hastily. "We'd better be going home."

Beth hadn't counted on the fact that she would be sitting in the front seat beside Ethan all the way home.

The children grew quiet and drowsy with the rocking of the car, and the silence hung heavy between them.

Finally Ethan spoke. "I hope you enjoyed the afternoon as much as I did." He glanced across the short distance, waiting for her answer.

"Yes, I had a wonderful time. And you made friends for life when you let the children steer the boat."

A deep chuckle rumbled from deep within him. "You have great kids, Beth." Lights from an oncoming car cast a flickering shadow across his face, and his voice took on a more professional tone. "How are the nightmares?"

The unexpectedness of the question caused Beth to hesitate for a split second before telling him the truth. "I'm still having them. I almost called you the night after Granny's dinner. That was a really bad one."

"Why didn't you?" he admonished.

"First of all, I couldn't find your telephone number. And by the time I found it, I felt I had things under control," she hedged. "Besides, I thought you needed your sleep . . ." Her voice trailed away feebly.

"Beth, it's part of a doctor's fate to be awakened in the middle of the night. I practice getting up just in case someone needs me," he drawled. "Next time, have the number handy, and don't worry about waking me. I'll just charge you double, if that will make you feel better. Agreed?"

"Agreed."

He dropped his lecture. "I was so glad to see you at church today. Did you enjoy the service?"

"Yes and no. I felt like a stranger, but I did learn I couldn't relive the funeral with all those happy people around." She sighed contentedly. "That was good. A growing-up thing. But," she added, "I found myself locked in an internal debate over the text the minister used."

"The 'You are Mine'?" His brows wrinkled.

71

"Yes." She crossed her arms over her chest in a gesture of protection—or defiance.

"You surely agree, don't you?" He began making the turn to her street.

"I don't think we have time for a full-fledged discussion tonight," she evaded. "We're almost home. Some other time—when we have an hour or two." Her faint smile begged indulgence. "Let's don't spoil the day with a theological debate."

"You're absolutely right," he agreed. The car rolled to a halt in the driveway. "I'll help you get the children into the house." He scooped up Sean effortlessly and headed for the front door.

Beth was right behind him with the sleeping Cally in her arms and quickly maneuvered the door open. "Just take him down the hall and to the left."

When the children were tucked into their beds, Beth motioned Ethan out of the room. "I'll undress them later."

On the way back to the den, she asked casually, "Would you like a cup of coffee?" She didn't know if she wanted him to stay or not, but she felt compelled to ask.

He was looking at her oddly, as if he were measuring something. "Thanks, but it's late, and I have a little reading to do." He was standing just outside the door now. "I was serious about your calling me if you need me. Anytime. Good night."

"I will. Good night. And thank you for a wonderful day."

As the door closed Beth felt a momentary pang of regret that she had not insisted he stay—at least long enough to finish their talk. *He couldn't have stayed anyway*, she reasoned. *He said he had some work to do*. She walked back to Cally's room and began slipping her clothes off. Buttoning the footed pajamas, her thoughts rambled on. *I wonder if he'll ask us out again?* As she readied Sean for bed, another thought

72

struck her. *I wonder if he'll ask me out again?* And she grinned into the semi-darkness.

During the next week Beth saw nothing of Ethan. She set up the children's swimming lessons and spent every morning at the pool with them. The afternoons seemed to evaporate in a whirlwind of unplanned housework. There was always just one more drawer to clean or one more closet to straighten.

Saturday morning she arose at her customary hour of six and took her coffee outside in the backyard to the swing under the hackberry tree. *Nothing in the world tastes as good as fresh coffee outside early in the morning,* she thought. The grass at her feet was still moist with dew. Birds chirped and sang as they gathered their day's fare. Beth smiled broadly as she watched a squirrel scamper across the grass and up a tree. *What shall we do today? A whole glorious day ahead of us and not one commitment to honor. I wonder if Granny really meant her invitation to lunch tomorrow. We should go to church again.*

The thought wasn't unpleasant, but there wasn't any excitement, either. Until she thought of Ethan. Carefully she held his image at arm's length while she looked at him. What was he in her life? Where did he fit? With great clarity she realized that he was nothing more than her doctor. In spite of their "date," their time together at Granny's, and the picnic with the children, never had he been anything other than professional with her. *And what about me? I am suspended between being married and single, and I still feel married. How long does it take to get over that feeling?*

It came like the first promise of spring after a hard winter—not quite there, merely a faint whisper—but a promise nonetheless. She realized suddenly that she wanted to be free of her marriage. The stunning thought struck her full force, causing some of the hot coffee to slide down the side of the cup. This time her smile was crooked. *I guess I've grown up another notch,* she thought before a soft desolation settled over her. Fingering her gold wedding band, she sighed. She was not ready to part with the symbol of her marriage yet.

I can't put all of it away. And what's more, I don't have to. We'll go to church tomorrow and then have lunch with Granny and Ethan and just enjoy being together. Who needs men, anyway? I've lived quite successfully by myself for two long years. How much better to have them just for friends—in case I need something. Beth smiled, knowing her thoughts to be half true—yet half wishing.

As the sun rose higher in the sky, the air began to crystallize into a metallic blue, losing the heaviness of the night. Beth's spirits rose, too, as she comtemplated the life that lay ahead of her. *I've been living one day at a time,* she decided. *It's time to start being who I really am. I don't have a husband. I do have a family to care for, a good responsible job. I have friends, and relatives who care for me. Maybe I'll take up golf. Maybe I'll give a party. I may even take the children on a long vacation somewhere.* She felt invincible, capable, in charge of her life. Confidence soaring, she walked briskly into the house and quickly showered before the children woke up.

She was frying bacon and flipping pancakes when Sean and Cally came bounding into the kitchen.

Sean wrapped his arms around her legs in a big good-morning hug. "Boy, does it smell good in here!"

"Hmmm, we're having a 'bration, aren't we, Mom?" Cally asked as she climbed up on the high kitchen stool.

"Yes, we are. We're celebrating Super Saturday. You guys sit down and have your juice. The food will be ready in one minute." The kitchen echoed with happy talk and mouth-watering aromas.

74

Carefully Sean poured the juice. "What are we going to do today?"

"What would you like to do?"

"Go to the lake with Dr. Stewart!" they chorused.

"And what's your number-two choice? We haven't been invited to number one."

Sean buttered a fluffy pancake. "We could practice our swimming."

"We could go see Granny," Cally said.

"We could, but I think we're having lunch with her tomorrow. How would you like to go fishing?" Beth asked.

"Do you know anything about fishing, Mom?" The doubt was plain on Sean's face.

"Honey, you're looking at a first-class fisherman. We could go out to the park and fish in the pond."

"Yeah, let's go fishing," decided Sean.

After breakfast Beth dug out the cane fishing poles from the back of the utility closet and they headed for the local park, stopping only for some fishing worms. Soon they settled in the shade of the huge old trees that ringed the pond.

"Are you going to put the worms on the hooks, Mom?" asked a doubtful Sean.

"Of course, all you have to do is ask them to be still for a minute," she teased.

Cally grimaced as Beth impaled the squirming worm with the hook. "Doesn't that hurt him, Mom?"

"I remember asking my father the same question. I wish I could remember his answer, Cally," she began patiently, "it's always icky-looking at first, but it's the only way you can catch anything. You have to use bait."

"But couldn't you use something that isn't alive? Maybe a candy kiss would be better."

Beth looked at the hopeful child. "I don't have any candy kisses. Here, drop this into the water and wait a minute. I saw some little sun perch here. Just pull the pole up if you feel something on your line." She baited Sean's hook for him as he took in every detail of the procedure.

As Beth had hoped, the concern over the worms' feelings were forgotten as soon as the first fish was hooked.

They spent a happy, giggly afternoon pulling in small perch. Each fish was finally returned to the water after a long explanation. Mentally Beth added, *and I don't have to clean them, either.*

They changed clothes and went out for a fish supper, pretending they were eating the fish they had caught that afternoon.

"This is the best part of fishing, isn't it, Mom?" said Sean, happily biting into the flaky fish.

They had barely walked into the house when the phone rang.

"Hello. Yes, Granny."

"You *are* coming tomorrow, aren't you, dear?"

"We'll be there. Thanks for asking."

"Church, too?"

"Church, too," she agreed.

"See you there. Got to run now. I have a pie in the oven."

Beth stood chuckling to herself as she hung up the phone. Then she got the children ready for bed and turned on the television set for them to watch a children's special. She was searching for the book she had started the night before when the phone rang again. "Busy night. Hello."

"Hi, I hope I didn't interrupt anything important." Ethan's resonant voice stirred some dormant emotion.

"No, the best part of the day has already been spent." She told him of their fishing expedition. Ethan laughed delightedly at Cally's suggestion of the candy kisses.

"You know, she may have something there. Maybe we ought to try it."

Beth heard the "we" part of the sentence, and in spite of her earlier decision, felt a small glow start somewhere in the middle of her chest. "Maybe," was her only reply to the implied fishing trip.

"Going to church and Granny's tomorrow?"

"There seems to be an epidemic of interest in that going around."

"Oh?"

"Granny called just awhile ago. Yes, we're going to church, and afterward to her house for lunch."

"Then may I come by and pick you up? It might simplify things."

"I don't know if it would simplify things—for you—but it would be nice. Cally wanted to sit with you last week. She'll be thrilled."

"Good. I'll be there around ten-fifteen. See you soon."

"Yes. Soon." As she replaced the phone, Beth wondered if this were going to be an every-Sunday arrangement. "It could be heading me down a dead-end street," she mused. "Or it could turn into something very interesting."

Ethan was late. In fact, he was very late. It was getting close to eleven o'clock, and she had not heard a word from him.

She tried to make excuses for him—a medical emergency, surely, maybe even an accident. But someone would have called her in either event. Then she got angry. She had just given up on him completely when she heard his car in the driveway.

"Sorry I'm late," he sang out as she opened the door. "I had an unexpected date at the emergency room. All ready to go?"

He didn't look contrite at all and Beth tried to hide

her frustration without any success. "For about forty-five minutes."

With proper meekness he said, 'I guess I should have called."

They climbed into his car, the children in the back, and Beth wishing she could join them.

"I am sorry, Beth." Ethan said. "I'm not accustomed to checking with anyone when I go to the hospital."

Weakly she responded, "It's all right. I'm not used to being stood up. Guess it's an occupational hazard."

"I promise to make it up to you."

He looked so earnest Beth couldn't help forgiving him. "That isn't necessary, Ethan. Forget it." But it felt nice, knowing he wanted to.

Sitting with Ethan and Granny in church gave Beth a strange sense of warped fantasy. They could be the average American family—husband, wife, children, grandmother. But Beth felt like a player in a charade. Though Ethan sat next to her, and she felt his warmth, there was no reason to feel the breathlessness that gripped her. He was totally involved in the sermon, oblivious to her. She tried to listen to the minister, but the scent of Ethan's after-shave kept coming between them. She changed postions in the hope of better concentration, but Ethan used the occasion to casually drape his arm along the back of the pew behind her. She could feel the pressure of his arm across her shoulders. The worst part of the entire thing was that Ethan had no idea what was happening to her. It was the first time she had felt that special maleness since Robert had died, and though it was totally innocent, the intimacy of it all made her dreadfully uncomfortable. Though she didn't move, she felt the need to escape. Inside, she was squirming. The picture of the worm at the end of Cally's hook flashed before her eyes. And though her danger was not as great, she vowed to use candy kisses from now on.

Vast relief flooded her when Ethan rose to help with the offering, and continued when he kept his arm by his side upon returning to their pew. He smiled as he sat down, and for a split second she could swear she caught a glimmer of mischief in that smile.

After the service Ethan carefully herded them all out the church door, and soon they were gathering around Granny's bountiful table.

The conversation was spirited and cheerful, but Beth found herself an observer rather than a participant. She watched Ethan with the children, noticed their total acceptance of him. She saw Granny waiting on them hand and foot, easing them gracefully through another feast.

When Granny again provided the opportunity to be alone with Ethan, he remarked, "You're very quiet today."

Beth took her place in the creaky old swing and smiled at his opening line. "Just thinking," she said noncommittally.

"Private thoughts?"

"Yes."

They moved to and fro until Ethan could think of another way to open the conversation. "What did you do with your first week of freedom?" It was a safe beginning.

"I enrolled the children in swimming lessons. It was nice getting up each day and going to the pool with them. They're both doing well."

"How long are the lessons?"

"One more week; then I'll have to find another activity for them. Any ideas?"

"What about a visit to your folks?"

"I haven't made any arrangements yet." Her eyes wandered over the sylvan scene stretched before them. "Robert's mom and dad usually want them for part of the summer."

"Will you go with them?"

"Not if I can avoid it." Seeing the surprise in his face, she added, "They were not overly thrilled with our marriage. They are good country people, and an educated daughter-in-law was difficult for them to accept. We just don't have anything in common except the children. One runs out of small talk in a hurry when there's nothing to discuss except ladies' magazine articles and recipes and little-known relatives." She turned to him. "That shocks you, doesn't it?"

"Not the information, but that you would share it with me. I never thought too much about in-laws— never had any reason to," he grinned. "But you don't get to pick them, do you?"

"No. Mine are good-hearted people, but we just never clicked."

"Why don't you send the children to them and take a short vacation for yourself?"

"Surely you jest."

"No, I'm quite serious. You could do anything your little heart desires."

"There's no way I could let those children out of my care, not even for a little while."

"Why not? Are your in-laws incapable of caring for them?"

She stirred uncomfortably. "No—but what if something happened to them? No, I couldn't take the chance."

"Are you afraid that if you aren't there to watch over them, they will be taken from you, too?" His voice was soft and gentle.

"There you go again! I thought you promised me you wouldn't be helpful unless I asked you to be. I'm not afraid. I'm just trying to be both a father and a mother—and, believe me, it isn't easy. I know a bachelor could hardly be expected to understand." As soon as the words were out of her mouth she regretted them, but it was too late.

"Probably not," he concurred.

She studied his face. Was he angry with her? At this point she didn't care one way or the other. Why was he trying to tell her how to live her life? She had asked for no opinions. He was supposed to confine his advice to her medical problems. And this definitely wasn't medical. She chanced another look. His expression was composed and serene. Maybe she hadn't made him angry at all. He knew it wasn't any of his business, so he probably didn't care. *But I doubt he'll bring up the subject again*, she thought with an inward grin.

"I'm sorry I snapped at you," she said with embarrassment. "You've been very kind to the children and me." Impulsively she added, "Let me atone. Come for dinner next week. I promise not to bark."

"It's a deal." His deep blue eyes warmed. "And I promise not to help . . . unless you ask."

It was hard to break the magnetic hold of his eyes on hers, but she struggled to move from the intimacy of the moment. Instinctively she knew it had been a mistake to ask him for dinner. It would throw them together again in another impossible situation, and she felt too vulnerable to walk this new tightrope of feeling on which she was balancing so precariously. *At least the children will be there*, she thought.

"Maybe we should check on the progress of the 'Go Fishing' game," she said aloud.

"All right."

They walked back to the house without further discussion.

The sound of laughter pealed across the lawn to greet them, and they heard Granny say, "Are you sure you two haven't been practicing at home? Why, I only have one card left!"

Exchanging grins, they entered Granny's happy home.

CHAPTER 5

SHE WAS WEARING A FILMY WHITE DRESS which floated about her bare ankles. Though her destination was uncertain, there was no feeling of fear. Rather, she seemed to be enfolded in summer's friendly arms, perfumed by the fragrant honeysuckle spilling in profusion from a nearby hedge. The sun warmed her face and thinly clad body and the earth beneath her feet. She could hear a hidden river playing its watery harp, and every bird seemed to be singing for Beth alone.

She was on her way to meet someone, and anticipation sped her steps as she hurried through the garden. Suddenly he came into view, and her only thought was to reach his side, for all the happiness in the world resided in that dear form. As she drew near, she could see the marvelous blue eyes, the russet beard. His mouth was curved in a wide smile of greeting, and he threw out his arms to her.

Ethan, too, was clad in white, chest bare and sun-warmed, and it was excitingly strong against her own as he wrapped his arms around her. As his lips descended to hers, she felt a flash of fire like summer lightning streaking through her. His hands tangled in the strands of her hair, pulling her closer to him, cherishing her . . . She could smell the sweetness of his skin, feel his silky beard against her face. And as she opened her eyes to look into the sea-blue of his, she caught sight of the man—the stranger. She opened her mouth to scream, to call out a warning to Ethan, but she succeeded only in pushing him off balance.

As they tumbled into space together, Beth felt the softness of the carpet beneath her, and she was lying on the floor of her own bedroom. Gasping for air, she lay perfectly still lest the man appear in her own safe room. Then, still locked in the horrifying mist of the dream, she struggled to her feet and fell heavily against the nightstand. Cruelly, she twisted the light switch and searched frantically among the pages of her address book for Ethan's number. With numb fingers she stubbed the numbers in their proper sequence, waiting breathlessly until she heard his sleepy voice.

"Ethan, help me!"

"Beth! Beth, are you all right?"

"No! Oh, Ethan, help me! He might come back! He might even still be here!"

"Beth, you're having another nightmare. Stop crying and listen." His voice was calm and soothing. "Turn on all the lights right now."

She dropped the phone and ran to the wall, flipping on the overhead light which promptly flooded the room. A frightened look around convinced her that here was no one there, and she picked up the phone, still gasping sobs.

"I'll be right over there. Stay where you are."

"No, no, talk to me! Don't hang up the phone! Just talk to me!" she cried.

Ethan made the comforting sounds a mother might

make to calm a frightened child. He wrapped her in them like swaddling clothes and verbally pulled her close to him.

"It was so bad, Ethan. It was so bad. I can't go on like this. You've got to give me something to make me sleep. I can't go to sleep at night, wondering if he's going to come again."

"I will," promised Ethan. "It's going to be all right. Now, tell me about the dream."

Instantly she was on guard, for there was no way she could confess the part he had played—that warm, impassioned embrace.

"It was the same," she said in a monotone. "The strange man was there again. I knew something bad was going to happen and that he wouldn't help me— he would just stand by and watch."

"Tell me exactly what happened," he commanded.

Determined not to reveal the details of the dream, she edited as she talked. "I was walking in a lovely garden . . . feeling very happy because I was on my way to meet someone, someone who cared for me. Just as we met, I saw the other man and there was a terrible sense of foreboding. Something was about to happen . . ." Her voice rose with remembered danger. "Maybe both of us would be hurt. We fell at the same time. It was the fall that woke me. In my struggle to escape, I fell out of my bed." Shame tinged her final words.

"Can you identify any of the other people in your dream?"

"No," she lied. "The others are irrelevant—it's the strange man who keeps coming back," she argued in exasperation.

"Beth, dreams are supposed to be symbolic of something—some inner personal turmoil—and if you can figure out the symbols, you can break the code. It's important, I think."

"I don't want to figure it out, Ethan, I just want to

go to sleep and not wake up until morning. Are you going to help me or not?"

The despair in her voice was heartbreaking. "Come to the office tomorrow and we'll see what we can work out. Will you be all right until then?"

"Yes," she answered tonelessly. "I can survive until then. Thank you for being there when I needed you."

"Come the first thing, will you?"

"Yes. I will," she promised. "I'll be fine, Ethan. Thank you again and good night."

He seemed reluctant to let her go, for he added, "And we *will* get to this bottom of this."

She hung up the phone without replying futher. It was only three o'clock—plenty of time to sleep before she had to be in his office. She straightened up the bed and cluttered nightstand and padded into the kitchen for a glass of milk.

Ethan had promised her they would find out the reason for her nightmares. There was hope. Hope, and a little fear. Fear of what? Ah, there was the mystery. Shivering slightly, perhaps from the cold milk, Beth went slowly back to her bedroom and tried to compose herself for sleep for the second time that night. With the promise of help in the morning, it was easier than she had thought it would be.

Hands shaky, Beth finished dressing. Earlier, she had arranged for Granny to keep the children for her, telling the older woman only that she had an appointment. Granny hadn't pried.

Beth dropped the excited children off on her way to Ethan's office, and in spite of her edginess, she felt a nudge of pleasure in seeing him again.

When she arrived she found that he hadn't yet come in from hospital rounds. His nurse seemed surprised to see her.

"He's expecting me," Beth explained feebly.

Mindlessly, she tried paging through the worn magazines, ultimately tossing them aside to watch a young mother trying to comfort a fussy infant. As the baby sneezed and coughed, Beth mused, *This is a good place to catch something*, and then thought of all the times she, too, had brought a sick baby into her doctor's office. Chuckling to herself, she thanked God that she was long past the seemingly endless stage in which this young mother found herself.

The nurse's rubber-soled shoes squeaked their way down the highly polished linoleum hallway, alerting Beth to the fact that the doctor was in and ready for his first patient.

"Mrs. Martin?" she called cheerfully.

This time Beth was taken directly to Ethan's office. *No need for the open-air examining gown this time*, thought Beth mirthlessly. With a deep sigh, she sank into the welcoming comfort of the wing chair facing his desk. Nothing had changed since her last visit—nothing in the room, anyway. But it was interesting to see this private room in view of what she now knew about the man. It still appeared impersonal—a professionally decorated stage.

She started slightly as the door opened suddenly and Ethan swept in, crisp and authoritative in his white coat.

He had her medical record with him and flipped it open on his desk as he took his place there. "Good morning. Were you able to get back to sleep?"

He sounded so clinical, but the smile was warm and honest.

"Yes, thank you." She gave him what she hoped was her best smile in return, but found it hard to maintain eye contact. Her pulse had speeded up and she felt a faint blush starting at her neckline and working its way up to her cheeks. She absolutely forbade herself to look at his mouth, the mouth that she had kissed with such abandon in her dream.

Surely he would be able to guess the significance of that blush.

"Feeling embarrassed this morning at having called me last night?" he grinned. "Please, don't." With great earnestness he looked deeply into her eyes. "I really want to help you, Beth."

She struggled with suppressed laughter which conveniently ended in a fit of coughing. "I'm sorry, Ethan. I'm a little off balance this morning." Now, *that* was the truth!

"Have you tried to fit names to any of the faces in your dream?" Patiently he waited for her answer.

It took her a second to answer carefully. "The main thing I need to know is the name of the stranger who refuses to help me. The others don't matter."

"But they do! Why are you fighting this so hard? There's nothing to be ashamed or embarrassed about. Believe me, I've heard just about everything there is to hear. Trust me, Beth." He was leaning forward, urging her with the very stance of his body.

"You say the people are symbolic of something of importance to *me*, so *I'm* the one who needs to figure this out. All I want from *you* is something that will guarantee me a good night's sleep," she shot back defensively.

"That's true. I can't make you share anything with me. After all, it is your problem." His obvious disappointment at her lack of trust in him carved a deep frown on his forehead.

"Please don't be angry with me, Ethan. I need time to think. I went back to sleep right away, and got up to hurry over here. I haven't had time to sort anything out yet. Help me now, and I'm sure I can give you the information you want later." Her eyes were large and wide, innocent of deceit.

"I'll help you this time, but on the condition that you honestly work toward a solution of your problem—if not with me, then with someone else."

87

Hastily he scrawled a prescription, tore the page from the pad, and pushed the small square toward her. "Promise." The set of his jaw was firm.

"I promise."

He rose to walk her from the office, taking her arm in a friendly way. "By the way, what day am I supposed to come to dinner this week?"

"Why, ah, how about Wednesday?" she stammered.

"Perfect. Six-thirty?"

"Yes, fine."

He waved a casual goodbye and was off to the examining room.

Beth walked down the hallway, shaking her head and muttering, "Out of the frying pan, into the fire. I'll need a good story by then." She began to chuckle, and the warmth that bubbled up within lasted intermittently all the way through the filling of the prescription.

The children wouldn't be through with their swimming lessons yet, so she decided to let Granny finish out the morning with them while she did her grocery shopping. She bought the special items she'd need for Wednesday night's meal in addition to her usual list and then ran a few more errands. Granny was already feeding the children lunch by the time she arrived to pick them up. At Granny's invitation, she joined them for sandwiches.

Beth kept her news to a minimum, which was fairly easy with the detailed account of the children's swimming prowess from their own lips, and Granny's nod confirming each story.

As the children wound down their recital, Granny managed to share some exciting news with Beth. "I'm going out to get an interview on tape tomorrow. Would you like to go with me?" Before Beth could answer, she hurried on to make the offer more attractive. "Why, the old couple must be in their late seventies. Should be real interesting."

Privately Beth speculated that Granny herself must be somewhere in her early seventies, and suppressed a smile of amusement.

"Why, they don't do anything but sit around and watch the weeds and their grandkids grow," Granny was saying. "There's so much they *could* be doing, but you know how some old folks are . . . Besides, I thought the children might like a chance to visit the country." She cocked her head at Beth speculatively. "About two o'clock?"

"That sounds great, Granny." What else could she say? She had practically promised Ethan she would accompany Granny on her lone trips to the country.

It proved to be an interesting afternoon, after all, and the children enjoyed being on a farm, even if it was no longer a working one. The buildings had been well-cared for, but the barnyard was devoid of any animals except for a faithful dog and a mother cat with kittens.

When Cally came in cuddling one of the mewing bundles of fur, Beth could not resist the plea in the wistful brown eyes. On the way home, the children were euphoric about their new pet; Beth, simply resigned.

Granny grinned delightedly. "I guess this trip didn't turn out quite the way you expected, dear." At Beth's shadowy smile, she added, "I did enjoy hearing those people talk about the olden days, didn't you?"

"Yes, Granny, I did. Uh, if you don't mind, I'll keep the tape and play it for Ethan Wednesday night."

Granny's sidelong glance was a knowing one. "Wednesday night?" she asked innocently.

"When Ethan comes to dinner." Quickly she added, "I owe him one for, well, never mind." But she didn't miss Granny's soft smile of pleasure. *I think I'm in over my head*, she thought. Sagely, Granny made no further comment.

Beth stood with a glass of water in one hand and the pills Ethan had prescribed for her in the other. She had been skeptical when she took them the first night, but they had indeed provided her with a restful night's sleep. She had awakened a little groggy, but grateful. Tonight there was no doubt she would have an equally restful night. But she knew once the bottle was empty she would be hard put to talk Ethan into more of them. The mere act of taking them was at best a Band-aid on a broken arm.

Thoughtfully she took both the bottle and the water with her to her bed and placed them on the nightstand. She crawled onto the bed and drew a small pad and pencil from the table, marking a careful ''1'' at the top of the page. Who could the man in her dream be? Clinically she searched her memory for details about the man, but try as she might, no firm image of him came to mind. He was a man with with obvious power—he knew she was in imminent danger—and while he was not directly responsible for the impending trouble, he steadfastly refused to rescue her. What *did* he look like? She could recall no distinguishing characteristics. He was only a nebulous form who appeared without warning—then stood silently, watching and waiting.

She measured him against the mental picture she held of her father, of Robert, of every man who had ever meant anything to her in her life. Shaking her head in frustration, she tried another thread. Why was she dressed in white, and barefoot? White might signify purity, or innocence. Could the bare feet mean defenselessness? In the dream she had felt totally vulnerable, armed only with fear to hasten her flight.

Restlessly she put down the pad and prepared for

bed. The pad still held only the number "1." The giant mental jigsaw puzzle she was trying to solve had too many missing pieces, and Beth felt she had exhausted the possibilities.

It was only as she was swallowing the pills that she allowed herself to remember she had not even considered Ethan's entrance into the dream. The corners of her mouth turned up involuntarily as she snuggled down into her pillow and recalled the full range of emotions she had experienced in that mythical kiss. Without fear of censure, she relived it one moment at a time, the intensity of those feelings undiminished, then gave herself up to sleep in the arms of Ethan Stewart.

As the time drew near for the real Ethan Stewart to appear, Beth felt strangely at peace. There were no pre-party jitters, no fear of his reading her eyes and knowing of her preoccupation with him. Purposefully reliving the dream last night had somehow erased the guilt.

If he does kiss me . . . she thought, and then stopped in dismay. *Listen to me*, she whistled silently. With a determined effort she changed her train of thought, but she couldn't halt the new feelings of womanliness that suffused her entire body.

And as she gave her short dark hair a final quick brushing, even Sean commented on her appearance. "You look pretty, Mom. Kind of soft or something."

It was Cally who got to the door first when Ethan knocked. And it was Cally who sat beside him on the couch while they waited for supper to be served. Her little-girl devotion was touching, stirring poignant memories for Beth. Sean regaled him with slightly inflated stories of their fishing expedition. But Beth made no attempt to shield Ethan from the large dose of domesticity to which he was subjected during the

91

happy evening. Nor did Ethan seem ill at ease with the love and attention the children showered on him.

Not once did he give any indication that he preferred to be alone with Beth, and even at his departure, it was the children who bid him the fondest farewell. It was only in the final seconds of the evening that he put his warm hand out to her, gently squeezing hers in a gesture of friendliness. It had been a perfectly lovely evening, and she felt not a trace of disappointment that they hadn't spent a single moment alone. For one thing, Ethan had not had an opportunity to question her further about her dreams. It was only after he was gone that she remembered the tape she had planned to share with him. *Later,* she promised herself.

The next day flowers arrived for her and candy for the children—a token of Ethan's appreciation for the enjoyable evening he had spent with them.

When the phone rang, she half expected it to be Ethan, and was completely surprised when it was her mother-in-law.

After the mandatory pleasantries, the older Mrs. Martin got down to the real reason for her call. "We'd like for the children to come and spend some time with us. Now, we know how busy you are, and we couldn't ask *you* to be away from your summer work that long, but we would like the children to come and stay for a month, wouldn't we, George?" There was an affirmative sound in the background as she hurried on. "Perhaps you could just put the children on the plane and we could meet them here. We could pay for their flight. Oh, it would be such an adventure for them, wouldn't it, George?" There was another grunt from Mr. Martin. "Now, don't be too quick to say no. Why don't you think about it and call us tomorrow night. Oh, do let them come, Beth. We miss them and Robert so much. It would mean so much to us to spend that time with his children, wouldn't it, George?"

At this point in the monologue, Beth was gritting her teeth. The tactlessness of her mother-in-law never failed to amaze her, but that was not reason enough to keep the children from her. Beth was feeling so good about everything that she broke into Mrs. Martin's conversation with George. "I think it would be a wonderful experience for them. I'll check the flight schedules here and call you tomorrow with the information."

"Why, Beth!" cried the astonished Mrs. Martin. "That's just wonderful! I had no idea . . . well, never mind. We'll look for your call tomorrow night." Apparently she had been braced for an argument, Beth thought grimly.

The children were eager to make the trip and immediately began planning what they would need to take with them, while Beth phoned the airline.

It was only in the darkness of her bedroom that night, when the quiet settled around her, that she realized the enormity of her deed. *This is what it will be like every night for a whole month. Total silence. What if the plane crashes? What if they get lost in the airport? What if they never come back to me?* A huge tear coursed over her cheek and sank into the greedy pillow.

Dear Lord, please don't take them from me, too, she begged with a desperation she had not felt since the day they had called her from the hospital to inform her Robert had been admitted. There was only One who had the power to make even large planes remain in the air, no matter the circumstances. And though He had not spared Robert, surely He wouldn't take her children from her. She must trust in His mercy.

It was a perfect day for flying, though, in the excitement of their adventure, the children scarcely knew the sun was shining. The novelty of preparing for the flight sustained them all the way to the boarding gate. It was only then that the realization hit them that Beth was staying behind. Sean was manfully brave, promising to take care of Cally. And Cally's single tear was whisked away with the take-charge manner of the friendly flight attendant. She pinned on their name tags and reassured Beth they would be under her personal supervision, promising to deliver them safely into the arms of their grandparents.

Amid hugs and kisses the children said their final goodbyes and Beth was left standing by the cold floor-to-ceiling window, watching the plane taxi down the runway. In the hope that they could still see her from the tiny windows, she waved until the plane had turned its tail and at last lifted gracefully off into the clear sky. But it was not until the huge jet was only a dot on the horizon that she left her post.

Beth couldn't ever remember feeling so alone. Even when Robert had died, she had the children to cling to and console. Now there was no one. Not even the possibility of seeing Ethan lifted her spirits.

She dreaded walking into the empty house. But once she had passed that hurdle, she flipped a cassette into the slot of the stereo for the comfort of Chopin and turned up the volume, plopping down into a nearby chair. It was as though a dark mist swirled about her, and she gave a strangled scream as something small and furry jumped into her lap, mewing pitifully.

"Oh, Hepzibah, you scared the life out of me!" she cried.

As soon as Beth touched the small ebony kitten, it began purring softly and curled up contentedly under her chin. Beth held the small animal against her cheek and began spilling all the tears she had so carefully stored. Quickly Hepzibah was awash in them. In spite of herself, Beth began to laugh. "It looks to me like you've had your first bath, cat." Big green eyes looked into her dark brown ones as she added, "I think you and I are about to become very close friends." In reply, the kitten reached out a small inquisitive paw and gently touched Beth's mouth.

It was delightful to have Hepzibah to talk to. Her kitten antics caused Beth to alternately laugh and despair of Hepzibah's ever growing up. Just having another body in the house was helpful, and taking care of her added immeasurably to the day.

The very first night the children were away, Hepzibah established her new sleeping place on the pillow next to Beth's. "Hmm, maybe we'll try this one time, but don't plan on its being anything permanent."

The second night Beth eyed the powder puff of black fur, tail curled around the tiny pink rosebud nose. "I should have remembered that pets very quickly begin to own their owners unless they stand firm," she mused aloud.

But she couldn't bring herself to shoo the sleeping kitten off her bed.

CHAPTER 6

ETHAN WALKED INTO his small apartment and tossed his car keys on the kitchen bar with a sigh of discontent.

Automatically he called his service to check for emergencies. Assured that no one needed him right now and hoping for one evening of peace, he mused on the rarity of that happening. But it would not be as rare as the evening he had spent in Beth Martin's home.

Seeing her there with her children had freed him to admit to the continuing bleakness of his existence. A glance around him provided ample contrast. A furnished apartment had seemed the practical thing at the time, but it was totally utilitarian, not homey. There were no deep-cushioned couches for lounging, no delicious aromas of home cooking wafting to greet him when he walked through the door each evening. No voices from the other room added laughter to his life.

His dreams of the clinic were real, but he couldn't shake the feelings of impermanence in his life. He moved between a decorated office and a furnished apartment. The void had become an ache.

Ethan stretched out on the couch and locked his arms behind his head, conjuring up Beth's image behind his closed eyes. *She was so nervous that first day in my office—so vulnerable.* Pretty ladies came and went through those doors, but none had been so appealing. He couldn't help grinning when he remembered the look on her face when he had suggested she might try falling in love again—or begin exercising! She was not weak-willed; she had stood her ground with him. But that very stubbornness could be one of the keys to unlock her anger.

He pondered the dilemma she faced. More than ever, she needed God's comfort, but Ethan was convinced she blamed Him for her husband's death. Certainly it was the most logical explanation, after spending only a short period of time with her. Unless she agreed to further counseling, however, he would have to proceed with that tentative diagnosis.

He longed to help her, but how could he gently guide her to an understanding and acceptance of her anger with God? Besides, it was a fact she must discover for herself before she would be ready to release it.

He swung his feet to the unremarkable carpet and sat at the edge of the couch, running his hands across his eyes and beard. Maybe he had made a mistake in going to Beth's place for dinner. *Rule Number One: Never become emotionally involved with a patient,* he reminded himself. How many times had he heard it? All through medical school, and again in his training to be a Christian therapist, it had been drummed into his head. "Love them, but don't fall *in* love with them—especially the attractive, vulnerable ones. Your goal is to help them to become independent, functioning adults," he repeated aloud.

He could appreciate the wisdom behind the edict. It

would be so easy to fall in love with Beth, and now that he had seen her and her children, he was hungry to know more about them. There was a chord deep within that little family he wanted to touch, to explore. He felt himself resonating to its harmony.

The camping trip hadn't helped things, either. He found himself watching for her, looking for unobtrusive ways to spend a little time with her. *But in order to help her, I do need to know her better,* he reasoned. *Careful, old man, careful,* warned a small inner voice.

Restlessly he prepared for bed and finally climbed between the sheets. *Lord, give me wisdom and prudence. If this woman is to be the part of my life I've waited for, give me the patience to endure. Help me to use all the knowledge I've acquired to show her the doors she must open, and grant her the strength to open and pass through them. I ask all this, trusting in Your plan for my life—and hers.*

Serenity came to him then, and so did Beth's face, smiling at him through his drowsiness. He gave himself up to sleep, comforted.

Later that week Ethan called her. "Must be quiet at your place with the children away. Granny told me."

"Well, there are no people noises, but I have a friend here who is trying to compensate," and she pulled Hepzibah off the dangling phone cord.

"I gather you have acquired a pet."

"I have acquired a bane and a blessing," Beth sighed, still pushing the playful animal away from the cord.

"And I was afraid you might be lonely."

"Ethan, you know how the Egyptians believed that people could be reincarnated into animals, especially cats? Well, I have living proof that it can happen. We named the cat Hepzibah for an Egyptian queen, and she is definitely a royal pain."

His laughter made her smile, too. "I thought you

98

might like to do something together tomorrow. The symphony is having a guest pianist. Care to get all dressed up and go with me?''

"That sounds wonderful. What time?"

"I'll pick you up around seven-thirty."

Roguishly she asked, "Is that a promise?"

"I see you give no quarter. Yes, it's a promise. See you very soon. Unless, of course, Mrs. Newman has her baby. 'Bye,'' he rang off cheerfully.

"Oh, you," she said into the dead phone. But her bright smile mocked her angry tone. "Hepzibah, you'll have to guard the fort by yourself. I'm off for a glamorous evening."

Feeling strangely young and giddy, Beth began her preparations for her date with Ethan early the next morning with an invigorating shower and shampoo. Then she very carefully selected the dress she would wear. One of her favorites, it was a long white gown that fell in soft folds from the tightly fitted bodice, leaving her arms and shoulders partially bare. She had purchased it because it reminded her of the soft Grecian gowns she had seen in a history book as a girl. Adding golden high-heeled sandals and gold jewelry gave her the finishing touches she wanted.

Too bad I don't have long blond hair. I could bind it up and be an exact replica of Athena. But then, wisdom is not exactly my forte right now, she admitted to herself ruefully. *Here I am planning to get all dressed up for a doctor who seems to have inoculated himself against feelings, and will probably leave me waiting while he runs to the hospital to perform a quick open-heart surgical procedure.* She laughed in spite of herself at the bleak picture she had created.

Hepzibah was ensconced on "her" pillow on Beth's bed and was licking herself, indifferent to her mistress's mental dilemma. Only when Beth sat down

99

beside her to smooth the kitten's silky fur did she respond with a contented purr.

"Cat, I guess it's silly of me to go out with him. And I am trying to be realistic about the whole thing. But I like being with him. And I need to get out of this quiet house. You're nice to have around, but you aren't the most scintillating conversationalist in the world. Nothing personal," she smiled. "You do help fill the days. There isn't anything left to clean in this house. Now it's on to something else."

Rising with a spring in her step, Beth began racking her brain for something worthwhile to do. There were a number of possibilities, but nothing really appealed to her. She prowled her personal library for a stimulating book, but she had read everything there. And her mind kept betraying her, racing ahead to the hours she would spend with Ethan.

When she opened the door for him, she was pleased to see Ethan quite handsome in evening dress. "You look wonderful!" She opened the door wider.

"You took the words right out of my mouth—though I would have chosen the word *gorgeous!*"

"And you're even on time." She attempted to ignore his compliment, though she could feel the warmth rushing to her cheeks.

Ethan pointed to his watch. "You will note that I am five minutes early."

They braved the crowd and found their seats, which were excellent ones quite near the stage.

After the first selection, as the artist was taking his bow, Beth said to Ethan, "I always wish I had worked harder on my piano lessons when I hear someone play like that."

"It wouldn't have done me much good, even if I had practiced twelve hours a day. The way that man plays is a gift." She nodded her agreement as the pianist again took his place at the huge concert grand.

100

Beth settled back to let the music sweep over her, carrying her into a tranquil, private place. The vibrant sounds stirred feelings of romance, and she felt her pulse begin to race with the quickening tempos. She was painfully aware of Ethan sitting beside her, of her bare shoulder next to the smooth texture of his coat. As the music wooed her, she could not resist looking at his strong hand resting on his knee. As desperately as a swimmer fighting a dangerous undertow, she fought the temptation to reach out and touch that hand. Giving herself a mental shake, she reminded herself for the umpteenth time that Ethan was her doctor, her friend—no more than that. Sighing, she willed herself to accept the role she was playing with him. *My friend. My dear friend.* A sudden surge of gratitude for that friendship came to her, and when he smiled at her, she was able to return his smile with a genuine one of her own.

During the intermission they visited with friends in the lobby, pointedly ignoring the curious stares of a few interested people.

As they took their seats once again, Ethan whispered, "You seem to be a hit tonight. Two of my friends have asked to be introduced to you." He grinned. "Better watch your step."

"Thank you for the warning, but I think the stares are more for the bachelor doctor."

As a patron of the arts, Ethan had been invited to the reception after the concert. Beth, too, was eager to meet the pianist, and when they arrived at the local hotel hosting the event, the ballroom was already crammed with well-dressed music lovers. The reception line moved them quickly along, and as they approached the virtuoso, a voice came from behind them.

"Hey, Fingers! Is that really you, Fingers?" A man glowing with enthusiasm was lunging for Ethan.

101

"Well, if it isn't the best trumpet player Plains High ever had! How are you, Wanderer?"

The two men grasped each other's hands in a warm handshake, then slapped each other on the back.

"Meet my best friend in high school, the Wanderer, or should I say Mark Glyns? This is my friend, Beth Martin."

Mark gave her an appreciative nod and turned eagerly back to Ethan. "Still play the piano? What times we had! People say we are still the best jazz band Plains has ever had."

"I thought you said you wished you'd done better with your piano lessons!"

"Oh, I do," Ethan confessed. "All I ever did was fool around with music. I never did get the hang of the really good stuff." Ethan's ears had turned slightly pink with embarrassment.

"Don't you believe it, Beth. He was one of the best. I was the one who just wandered around until I found out what key we were in. Ethan was the star of the show." He poked a playful finger at Ethan. "I bet you're making a living doing something with those talented fingers."

Beth and Ethan burst into laughter. "You're right!" Beth replied. "He went to medical school and became a doctor!"

"I should have guessed. Well, I wander no more. I'm in real estate." His chest heaved with a nostalgic sigh. "I miss those days sometimes. Working up a new chart for us when we can get together to do a little jamming."

"Ouch! Please don't say 'chart' to an off-duty doctor," Ethan chided.

"Sorry, pal. I'm here visiting my sister, but we need to get the old gang together sometime. It was good to see you, Ethan."

"Good to see you, Mark. Keep in touch."

"Hey, Beth," Mark leaned over and whispered loudly, "get him to play for you sometime."

"Hmmm. I'll do that. Goodbye, Mark," she called as the effervescent fellow moved off to greet another old-time friend. She turned to Ethan. "You will, won't you—play for me, that is?"

"Probably not even on my best day. That's ancient history. And if you ever tell a living soul my nickname in high school was 'Fingers,' I vow I'll never speak to you again!"

Beth suppressed a giggle just in time to be introduced to the soloist of the evening.

After the amenities, Ethan steered her to the punch bowl where they visited with other mutual friends. But it wasn't long before he pulled her aside. "I think we've made the rounds. Ready to go?"

"I suppose so, but what interesting people we've met tonight, 'Fingers.'" She cocked her head and gave him a mischievous grin.

"Let's get out of here." He frowned ferociously and responded by taking her arm. "Since the evening is still young, why don't you introduce me to your new roommate." By now he looked a bit like a college freshman asking for his first date.

"You asked for it! But at least you're wearing black. The cat hair won't show on your evening clothes at all," she retorted.

Later, Ethan followed Beth around the kitchen as she made the coffee. Hepzibah watched every move with great green eyes.

"I think you may have a genuine watchcat," he observed. "She hasn't taken her eyes off me since we got here." He reached down and patted the kitten, causing her back to arch and her tail to curl up high over it. The friendly gesture was a mistake, for Hepzibah rubbed herself against his black pants in delicious pleasure and moved in and around his feet in peril of being stepped on. When Ethan sat down she hopped confidently into his lap. "No, cat, this is where the friendship ends," he growled, and pushed her off.

Beth picked up the errant cat and closed her up in the bedroom. "Pushy little thing, isn't she?" she said as she sat back down with her coffee.

They were seated in the living room on the pale blue velvet couch, sharing their steaming cups of coffee and friendly glances.

"It was nice of Mrs. Newman not to have her baby tonight," Beth said.

"I told her it was an unlucky day to have a child."

"Ethan, do you believe in luck?" Her face was too serious for him to treat the question lightly.

"Actually, I don't. I believe everything is part of God's overall plan."

"You think He plans the bad things that happen to us?"

He leaned forward slightly. "No, but He *uses* them. It is our choice whether we allow them to make us stronger or to estrange us from God."

Relaxing against the soft cushions, she said, "I don't think I have turned away from Him. But to be honest, I do feel like I'm on hold. I know He's there, but He seems so far away right now." Her face clouded. "I feel my prayers must get hung up in the light fixtures."

"He's answering your prayers."

"I beg to differ," she said sharply.

"Sure He is. You know the three answers He gives—yes, no, and wait awhile. You do the same thing to your children. You don't give them everything they want when they want it, do you?" At her negative nod, he continued. "Neither does God. Sounds like you're in a wait-awhile pattern."

"What do I do in the meanwhile?"

"Patience, patience, patience. Gives you character," he said a bit flippantly.

"You did it! You finally did it. You gave me one of those canned answers I hate so much! Oh, Ethan, how could you? You're the one person I thought would never throw me one of those dry bones."

His acute embarrassment at her disappointment was evident. He hung his head momentarily. "*Mea culpa*. I have sinned greatly."

"Yes, you have, and a phony confession won't get you off the hook. Character! I'm really surprised."

"Let's not let this get out of hand. What I said is true, and you know it. You're just mad because I reminded you of it instead of giving you some new and greater truth. Well, there isn't one greater than the fact that you will have to grow during this time." He watched her put down the cup of coffee in great agitation. Reaching for her hand, he said softly, "It's been a long dry spell for you, hasn't it?" She nodded a miserable yes. "I've been there, too. When that happens to me, I read all of David's angry psalms."

"Oh?"

"David seesawed between total trust in God and anger, and when things didn't go the way he thought they should, he'd rail against God. I like that; it gives me comfort. In the end he'd always go back to Him, but he was never shy about complaining."

"That's not the way I remember the psalms. Wasn't David always praying for strength and praising God."

"Read them with new eyes. He began a lot of them with, 'Hurry up!'" At her skeptical frown he quoted, "'How long, O Lord? Wilt thou hide thyself for ever?' He wasn't a patient man." Ethan sighed.

"Are you sure you're quoting those songs right?" The doubts were clear on her disbelieving face.

"It's fascinating." Ethan warmed to his subject. "His poems pretty well follow a pattern. He complains impatiently, reminds God of His promises, and then praises God for what he expects Him to do. David had such a close friendship with God that he felt he could remind Him whenever he felt God had let him down."

"I still think you're way off track." Her eyebrows crinkled in concentration, but it was difficult to argue with Ethan's quotations. Beth thought for a moment. "I apologize about the dry bone comment. You really outdid yourself this time in outrageous concepts."

"I thought you said you didn't like people who play games with you," he said practically. "That's healthy, you know. My practice would be way down if folks were honest with each other."

She laughed. "Yes, and the murder rate would be skyrocketing."

His chuckle was rumbly and warm. "I'm afraid you're right. Beth," he said, causing her to look into that kind face only inches from her own.

"Beth, we won't ever play games. You're a rare person."

She felt a warmth start in her face and travel pleasantly throughout her body. Her dream seemed to be coming true. Ethan was so close that she could feel his breath against her cheek. She wanted to reach up and touch the golden-red beard. For a millisecond she feared the appearance of the man in her dream, but she knew she was wide awake and that Ethan was about to kiss her. She felt her eyes grow heavy-lidded, and her mouth parted slightly in anticipation.

But Ethan was moving away from her, looking at his watch. "I had no idea it was so late," he muttered. "I'd better check my answering service and see if Mrs. Newman has called in." He rose quickly, moving toward the door. "I didn't wear my beeper tonight. Afraid it would to go off during the concert."

Dazed, Beth followed him to the door, wondering if this could be a variation of her nightmare.

Formally Ethan said, "I had a wonderful time tonight, Beth. Tell the children hello for me when you talk to them next."

"Yes. Of course. I had a lovely time, too. Good night," she called to his retreating figure.

"Good night," he echoed over his shoulder.

Shutting the door, Beth leaned heavily against it in complete puzzlement. "I hope he does a better job of delivering babies than he does understanding women."

Hepzibah was waiting for her in the bedroom, purring loudly on the bed. She watched expectantly for the customary caresses, alert for any signs that playfulness might be tolerated. But Beth walked distractedly by Hepzibah and stood at her dressing table. Placing her jewelry in its case, she glanced in the mirror and, seeing the care she had taken with her dress and make-up, felt foolish.

She blushed as she remembered how ready she was for Ethan's kiss. She tried so hard to intellectualize the entire event, but became hopelessly entangled in her emotions.

With purposeful strides, she went to the bathroom and quickly took the medicine Ethan had prescribed for her. "I hope there is only barely enough time to get ready for bed," and she raced the effect of the pills.

Just before drifting off to sleep, she wondered idly what she was going to do when the magic pills were gone.

Hunched over Granny's kitchen table, Granny and Beth listened intently to the tape of the couple they had recently interviewed. At its conclusion, Granny said, "That will be a good one for the library."

"What happens now?"

We'll take it down there and get it catalogued and let the librarian put it in the collection. I hope Ethan can get a good photograph of them, too." Granny opened the refrigerator and removed a frosted pitcher of tea. "There's mint on the counter."

They chose to have their refreshing drink in the garden swing. Sitting where she and Ethan had spent pleasant times together made Beth slightly uneasy.

"How are you and Ethan getting along?" At Beth's startled look, Granny explained, "I'm too old to be tactful. Well?"

"He's very nice. And we always have a good time together."

"A real flaming romance, huh?" Granny took a big swallow of tea and waited. When Beth refused to enlighten her further, she tried again. "What's the matter, darling?"

Beth examined her frosted glass. "I have no idea. The other night I thought, well, I thought for a minute he was going to kiss me, but . . ."

"Maybe I ought to mix him up a spring tonic. Beth, how do you feel about him?" She placed her work-worn hand over Beth's limp ones.

"I honestly don't know, Granny. He's one of the finest men I've ever met. I know he likes me. And he's crazy about the kids. Granny," her eyes narrowed, "maybe that's it. He doesn't want a ready-made family. He likes all of us, but he told me once, he likes giving children back when the're cross or dirty. He doesn't want the full-time responsibility of a family."

"Pshaw. When a man's in love, he's in love, and two wonderful children couldn't possibly stand between him and the one he loves. What is the matter with that man? Maybe I ought to have a talk with him."

"Granny, don't you dare! I absolutely forbid you to say one word to Ethan about any of this!" The fear in her heart flashed out through the eyes. "Promise me you won't!"

"All right, but I hope I don't regret the day I made this promise," she said grimly.

At home in the quiet of the sultry evening, Beth

reflected on the conversation she had shared with Granny. What was the reason for Ethan's acting like a school boy with his first girl? He had been jaunty about his other "near misses" of marriage that day on the lake. She dredged up all the information she could recall his sharing on the subject. There wasn't any more.

"Maybe I need to face the fact that Ethan Stewart doesn't want to get seriously involved with anyone. At least not with me," she grimaced to her ever-present furry companion. With a growing confidence, she continued, "What do I care? I have no intentions of getting involved, either. I've just recently decided that I'm single again. Women don't have to be married to find fulfillment these days. Look how well I've done without a man in my life," she said smugly. "Now that I think about it, I have my whole life ahead of me. It's definitely my market." And she thought about all the handsome men she had seen at the concert and smiled.

Sunday morning found Beth settling in a pew on the other side of the church from the one she had shared with Granny and Ethan the week before. She scanned the congregation—really looking at the people for the first time. The bulletin noted a meeting of the singles' club the following week, and she toyed with the idea of going. There was one thing that troubled her, though. What would she do if Granny invited her to lunch again today? *I can't hurt her feelings, but I don't want to spend another captive afternoon with Ethan. It all seems so futile.*

She thought about the discussion she had had with Ethan about the Psalms and turned in the hymnal to a section of selected Psalms. It was alarming how many of them fit the description Ethan had given them. They did sound pushy and demanding. *Funny, I never noticed that before*, she thought disconcertedly. But she found strange comfort in the challenging tone of David's songs to his God.

I never think of God in that way. Christians are supposed to accept God's will for their lives, aren't they? Her brow crumpled in the confusion of her thoughts. *When His hand is heavy on me, I must remember to humble myself to Him. I have no right to complain at the way my life is turning out. Obedience. I must learn to be obedient.*

She listened to every word of the sermon, searching always for new ways to dedicate her new life to God. Maybe there would be a clue of some kind, giving her an idea of how to bend her will to His. The text, based on Jesus' Sermon on the Mount expanded her thinking rapidly.

As the minister read the Beatitudes, she could readily identify with some of them.

"Blessed are the poor in spirit . . ." he intoned.

That's me, all right.

"Blessed are those who mourn, for they shall be comforted . . ."

When, Lord?

"Blessed are the meek, for they shall inherit the earth . . ."

I hear You. I'm going to practice meekness, honestly.

By the time he finished reading the entire section, she was sitting stock-still. Everything in his sermon directly contradicted what Ethan had told her about David's Psalms and wrestling with God. But Ethan was not a minister. And the minister had read Jesus' own words. Jesus was meek. David was only a man, and one who had done a lot of sinning, if she remembered her Old Testament. *Lord, help me to be a humble and obedient servant,* she prayed at the end of the sermon.

Her first test came immediately.

"Good morning, Beth," cried Granny. "I hope you're planning to come over for lunch."

How can I possibly hurt her feelings? She's old and she means well. I don't want to go. Panic gripped her as she thought about being stuck with a man who had no purpose in her life now. Recalling what she had so recently prayed, she said, "How nice, Granny. I wouldn't miss it."

And, of course, Ethan was there, cheerful and entertaining. *You don't give a person much time to get her feet planted, do You, Lord?* She set her jaw and decided to have a good time. But before it was all over, the good time had a hollow ring to it. Without the children to enliven things and divert all the attention to themselves, the meal had a definite drag.

"Now you two just go on down to the garden while I clean this little bit of mess away. Go on, now, scoot!" She shooed them out the door.

Unwilling to follow their usual pattern, Beth headed for the small lake that lay at the back of Granny's property. There were fluffy ducks lazily paddling along, suddenly turning their pointed tails into the air like crazy toy animals upended by a careless child. Their plunge to the bottom of the lake in search of food made Beth smile.

The air was so laden with moisture it made breathing difficult. But the rain-swollen clouds to the south resolutely marched around the edge of the city, giving away only the smell of rain. How she longed for a cooling shower.

Ethan headed for an old pier that rakishly pushed out over the water. "Don't worry, it's safe," he said, noticing her hesitation. " I fish here sometimes." As they settled down on its creaking planks, he added, "Look, there he is," and pointed to a large catfish almost motionless in the sunlit water. "I've tried to catch that monster for two months. Used every bait Granny has suggested."

"Why don't you just use a net and pull him in? He's close enough to touch right now."

"Beth, that's not fishing. That would be as unethical as shooting a quail on the ground. No, when I finally catch him, it will be as a fisherman. He deserves to be caught honestly."

"Have you tried candy kisses?"

His laugh was so pleasant she found herself looking at the forbidden area of his mouth. He was so achingly handsome with the sunlight dancing in his hair, his mouth slightly open in laughter. The merriment she saw in his eyes was more than she could bear, and, in self-defense, she looked at the comical ducks bobbing in the distance.

"How are you doing with your nightmares? Are you working them out?"

She could feel his direct gaze on her face. "Yes, I am. Only this morning I think I made a real start." She faced him honestly, looking into those eyes that seemed to capture her very heart. "Ethan, I've made a promise to God, to be more faithful and humble and to learn how to be an obedient servant."

He frowned. "The role doesn't fit you." It was a flat, unequivocal statement. When she said nothing in defense, he went on. "You are not the subservient type. You're a woman who wants to know how, when, and especially why. If you persist in trying to be something you're not, it will only lead you into more trouble."

"First of all, *Doctor* Stewart, I'm not in trouble, as you so charmingly phrased it. I only have a little trouble with nightmares. And secondly, because I am the type of woman you describe, it's important that I learn that God knows how, when and especially why. He'll let *me* know when it's time." She saw the creases across his forehead, carved by his frown. "Ethan, you may not agree with me, but let me try this. I think it will work for me." With her eyes she begged his indulgence, for she had one more request. "I also need more time. I'm feeling my way slowly, but I *am* trying. I need you to give me one more prescription for sleeping pills." She rushed on before he had a chance to refuse. "I promise I'll not ask for more, but you did say work this thing out. I can't do it in one night. Give me some more time."

All that she could hear was the silence following her plea. Ethan was gazing out over the small lake, his eyes narrowed against the glare of the sun, or was it with worry? Beth held her breath while he wrestled with her request. She read the compassion in his eyes as he turned to her.

"All right. One more. But that is positively the last one."

"Thank you, Ethan." They were sitting close together in the muggy heat and, though the pier was sheltered by the shade of statuesque old oak trees, it was uncomfortably warm. Beth hadn't notice how warm until a slight breeze from the passing clouds rippled coolly across the lake. They sat together in companionable silence, watching the catfish bask in the sunlit side of the pier.

Beth tried not to look at Ethan, but felt his closeness and smelled the special maleness of him, heightened by the sun. She was becoming aware of his every breath, the beauty of his healing hands, so close to hers on the rough plank of the dock. Abruptly she stood, unable to bear the closeness a moment longer.

As soon as she stirred, Ethan rose with her, and in so doing the movement put them face to face on the narrow planking. He looked down into her eyes, and with great tenderness kissed her lightly on the mouth. Sliding his arm around her small waist, he pulled her close for an instant, then released her and stepped back for her to pass.

It all happened so quickly, so unexpectedly, that Beth had no time to assimilate the reality of the event.

She had dreamed about this happening, but now that it had, she wasn't sure what to do. But her body did. Her legs felt rubbery and her heart was pounding mercilessly. She felt giddy and astonished and joyous.

They walked back toward the house, Ethan's hand on her arm guiding her gently. Nothing was said. When the screen door slammed, Granny called out, "Anybody ready for ice cream?"

"Sounds good to me," Ethan said in a cheerful voice.

They sat outside on the screen porch on the shady side of the house overlooking the sloping green grass and stately old trees. If Granny noticed the high color in Beth's cheeks, her face didn't reveal it.

It was Granny who told Ethan about their trip to the country for the taping of the "old folks," as she called them. "Would it be possible for you to get a good photograph of them?"

"Certainly."

"Well, I have too many things to do this week to go back out there. But Beth could show you the way, couldn't you, dear?"

"I-I guess so, but it really isn't that hard to find."

Granny played it to the hilt. "But you already know them. They might give a strange man a hard time. You'd better plan to go out there with him. We wouldn't want him to get blasted with a shotgun or anything."

"You might as well give in. You're stuck with me," Ethan winked. "Let's make it next Wednesday. Okay?"

"Sure. I guess I'd better drive so you won't get lost." She couldn't resist the gibe.

"I think you two should go home and let an old lady get her afternoon nap. Don't worry about the dishes. I'll work it into my schedule for tomorrow. Now run along."

Ethan walked Beth to her car. "I think she was trying to get rid of us, don't you?"

"Yes, but she's so subtle I don't always catch on. I'll pick you up about nine o'clock. We don't want to get caught in the woods after dark."

Ethan shut her door. "I'll bring some camping gear just in case. We can practice for the next camp-out."

As she drove down the street to her own home, Beth marveled at the things that had transpired in the past few hours.

Is this your way, Lord, of telling me that I am on the right track? I was meek and went to Granny's. She didn't remember what Granny had served for lunch, but every scene of the drama played out on the pier was firmly etched in her brain. And Ethan's light kiss permanently marked her mouth.

Doctors don't kiss their patients, she reasoned. *Maybe I do mean more to him than he's let me think. Otherwise, why did he kiss me? Well, it wasn't a passionate kiss, but it was a kiss. There was tenderness in it, and respect, and compassion.* Did he feel sorry for her in her struggle against the awful nightmares? Beth's brain was reeling with cross-information. But one thing seemed clear. As soon as she had made an honest effort to be meek, Ethan had kissed her for the first time.

All the next day Beth practiced meekness. She let the rude woman shopper cut in line in front of her, and even forgave her on the spot. She didn't get angry when the driver of a car almost hit her in a stupid driving mistake. She didn't yell at Hepzibah when the foolish cat knocked over an entire quart of milk on the cabinet, where she shouldn't have been in the first place. She listened patiently to an unsolicited telephone promotion that got her out of the bathtub, and answered in a sweet voice, refusing the outlandish offer. By the end of the day, she was feeling solid with gentle righteousness.

Tuesday's test was a little harder. She telephoned the children, but spent most of the time talking to her mother-in-law. There were only a few precious minutes that she could spend with them, and rejoiced to find them obviously happy and busy. She chose the best part of the conversation to remember and savor, blocking out Mrs. Martin's tiresome chatter.

That night Beth went to sleep with their lilting voices echoing in her mind, seeing each of them, small and dear.

On her way to pick up Ethan the next morning, she felt positively cheerful, knowing whatever happened that day was in God's plan for her.

As she drove up in front of his house, she didn't see his car. *Probably in back.* When he failed to open the door to her insistent ringing, she felt the rise of anger. *No, I won't get mad. He'll be here shortly. He knew we were going to the country today. He'll be here. It's his day off; maybe he just ran out to get something.* She went back to her car and practiced waiting patiently.

Beth tried keeping her eyes off the small wrist watch on her arm. At the end of a long thirty-minute wait, she decided to drive down to his office. As soon as she saw the deserted parking lot, she lost the battle against anger.

He did it to me again. Just disappeared. No note, no phone call, no nothing. Her face was flushed, and she was mad, mad, mad. *How could he?* All he had to do was pick up the phone. *I've never met such an irresponsible man! He's not accountable to anyone.*

She drove back home, almost enjoying the totality of her rage. Changing into a ragged pair of jeans and an old shirt, she went into the back yard and began cleaning out flowerbeds. It was more than three hours before she heard her front doorbell ring.

Sauntering through the cool house, she was in command of her feelings again.

"Oh, Ethan. How nice of you to drop by." Her voice was pleasant, almost friendly.

Miserably he said, "Mrs. Newman's baby came this morning. I'm so sorry about our date."

"What date? Oh, no, don't tell me today was the day we were supposed to go out to the farm! I completely forgot about it. I was so eager to get the flowerbeds cleaned. Well, it doesn't matter. Come on in and have a glass of tea."

Ethan looked at her carefully, trying to decide what was happening. "You forgot?"

She turned away to get the glasses from the cabinet, guilt compounding her sins of the day. "Do you use sugar?"

Ethan sat down at the table. "Yes."

When she met his eyes at last, her gaze was level. Only a slight trembling of her hand holding the glass betrayed her. "Tell me about the baby and Mrs. Newman. Are they all right?"

"Yes, fine. Eight-pounder. A boy, thank goodness. She already has two girls." They sat across the table, sipping from the icy glasses. "Beth, let me try to explain. When the hospital called saying she had gone into labor, all I could think about was getting there to be with her. She had a terribly difficult delivery last time, and I wanted to be sure I did all the right things." His eyes shone with inner joy. "There is nothing in this world that is as exciting to me as delivering a baby. Fighting, with the mother, to bring a new life into the world. It's scary and joyful at the same time. The first time I hear that little bundle of squirming flesh cry, I get cold chills all over my body. No matter how many babies I deliver, it's always the same. I feel so . . . so victorious."

117

His face was glowing with happiness, and there was no way Beth could be angry with him any more. She put out her hand, touching his across the table. "Ethan, I didn't forget. I was mad that you hadn't taken time to let me know something had come up. But when I see you like this, I'm ashamed of myself for reacting so selfishly." She sighed deeply. "Being human, though, I'll probably get just as mad the next time."

They shared a laugh and sat looking at each other contentedly.

"Is there still time to go out to the farm?" Ethan asked.

"No more babies to deliver today?"

"Nope. I'm at your command. I even left my beeper at home."

"Okay. I'll change and be ready in fifteen minutes." At his doubtful look she added, "Well, twenty. If you're hungry, there's food in the 'fridge."

The trip to the country was off to a cheerful start and Beth was surprised at how quickly they reached their destination. The elderly couple remembered her, inquired about her cat, and posed in a dignified manner for Ethan's camera.

"That was a pleasant mission," he remarked as they returned to the car. "Do you have any other plans for the afternoon?"

"No. What did you have in mind?"

"There's a lovely little river not too far from here where we could while away the hot afternoon."

"You drive."

They stopped just short of the sandy bank and took an old blanket from the back of the car to spread on its inviting contours.

Ethan brought his camera from the car to the rippling stream. "I've been fishing here a few times. Too bad we don't have any tackle."

118

They settled down to enjoy the cool shade and soothing country sounds.

Beth felt her skin tingle with the joy of the intimate setting, and memories of Ethan's recent kiss were all too vivid.

"Would you mind if I took some pictures of you?"

"I suppose not. Just make sure they're flattering."

He gave her instructions to move this way and that and seemed satisfied with the several shots he made. He put the camera down and stretched out on the blanket, sighing. "This is the way to spend the day. No phones ringing, good company, and no patients."

"I'm a patient," she reminded him.

"Yes and no. I think of you more as a friend now."

Her body sent out a prickling alert. "I think of you as a friend, too, Ethan." She tried not to look at his peaceful face, eyes closed against the summer sun; tried not to remember how his mouth had felt on hers—and failed.

Ethan opened his eyes as she moved to the safety of a towering old water oak, then followed her, leaning beside her against its gnarled trunk.

He took her hand and held it rather carelessly, idly following the contours of each finger with a gentle touch. Mesmerized, she watched as he moved the hand to his mouth, kissing the fingertips methodically. Then he leaned closer and brushed his lips over hers. It was a tender kiss that left her spiraling. He drew back and looked long into her eyes. She tried not to fall into the cool blue pools. Breaking their gaze, she looked out toward the singing river. Was it singing for them? Ethan had not spoken a word, using his mouth and hands and eyes to speak for him. But Beth was not sure what they were telling her. There were no declarations of love, no promises.

"Ethan."

"No, Beth, don't say anything. I just want to be your friend. I care for you a great deal. I enjoy your

119

company, but these last few moments haven't placed any permanent bindings on our friendship."

"You mean this is just a pleasant way to pass an afternoon." The statement was flat, without feeling. "I think I want to go home now, Ethan."

"Please don't be angry. You looked so enticing here by the river, I couldn't resist. You're a very attractive woman, you know." He looked away. "I'm sorry if I took advantage of the romantic time and place." Without another word he stood up and pulled her up after him. They shook out the blanket and climbed back into the car.

They drove in silence, but there was a riot of words careening through Beth's head. *It didn't mean anything. He just got carried away. Romantic time and place. Don't be angry. Friends.*

She held back the tears of frustration and rage all the way to his house. As he stepped from the car, she said, "I don't kiss casually or for entertainment. Goodbye, Ethan." She backed out the driveway the instant he shut the door, not looking back to see how he had responded to her pronouncement.

Her mouth was a hard, bitter line, held firmly until she reached the privacy of her bedroom. There it dissolved into a flood of tears, washing away all the lovely memories of an idyllic afternoon.

Hepzibah jumped on the bed with her and licked her lifeless hand. Beth pulled the mewing kitten to her as she curled up on the bed.

" It must be time for your next bath, cat. But I can promise you, it will be the last one you get from tears shed over Ethan Stewart."

120

CHAPTER 7

IN THE NEXT FEW DAYS. Beth deliberately stayed away from the house as much as possible. She called friends and went to lunch, shopping for hours at a time, walking the huge shopping mall, returning only in time to take a sleeping pill and fall into a deep, dreamless sleep. She phoned the children often and spent one afternoon at the library, listening to the tapes Granny and Ethan had donated. She lost herself completely in the early history of the area, reliving with the pioneers the hardships and joys of establishing a new life.

How much simpler their lives were then. All people had to do was to survive. There seemed little time for interpersonal entanglements. No time for senseless games and façades.

Well, Lord, You seem to want to humble me, and here I am again, knocked to my knees. What is it You want for my life? I thought You were telling me something about Ethan. An unconscious sigh escaped her. *Maybe I'd be better off without him. He is so dedicated to his patients that he'd probably never remember to come home or even call to let me know*

121

where he'd be. You know best, Lord. Maybe You're trying to spare me years of frustration.

Beth had been so involved in her discussion with the Lord that she failed to see a patient librarian trying to get her attention.

"Mrs. Martin, are you all right?" The woman's wide eyes were magnified even larger by her concern—and her tortoise-shell glasses.

"Oh, yes, of course."

"If you're finished with that tape, I'll take it. Mr. Stanley has been waiting quite awhile for you to finish."

Beth endured the teacherish reprimand, but gathered her things together and left the library in as dignified a manner as she could muster. "I thought things were supposed to be slow and easy in a library," she muttered through clenched teeth.

She sat in her car for a few minutes, trying to decide whether or not to go back home. She dreaded the thought of the ringing telephone, for Ethan would definitely try to make amends. He was always trying to patch up something or someone.

The blazing summer sun made the car unbearably hot, so she started the motor, still undecided. But at the least the air conditioning made the waiting easier.

Maybe I should fly up and see the children. This town is getting too small. But even as she formed the thoughts, she rejected them, for just the idea of spending even a few days listening to her mother-in-law made home seem infinitely more desirable. *It's stupid to try to keep dodging Ethan like this. I might as well let him make his pitch and get it over with.* So she drove home and spent the afternoon and evening waiting for the phone call that never came.

Now that she had made up her mind to let Ethan off the hook, she wanted it to be soon. Once, she even picked up the phone to be sure it was operating.

Very late in the evening she decided to take a

shower, knowing that was a sure way to get the stubborn instrument to ring. Even that didn't work.

It wasn't until she reached for the empty bottle of sleeping pills as she prepared for bed that she realized her true predicament. When she told Ethan goodbye, had that meant only their personal relationship, or did it include their professional one as well? *How can I go to him now and ask for more pills?* She could still see his stern face as he gave her "this last prescription." There was no point in even asking. No, she would have to tough it out—and tonight was the night she must begin.

All I have to do is clear my mind, think pleasant thoughts, and relax. She reached into the back of her dresser drawer and brought out a shimmering nightgown, one she hadn't worn for a long time. Blocking out any remembrance of the last times she had worn the gown, she donned it and sat before her dressing table, brushing her hair. Carefully she sprinkled bath powder on her sheets and reached for her favorite book of poetry. She was comfortably propped in the most pleasant surroundings she could devise, and began to read from the slightly tattered book.

She chose only the verses she loved best, and soon felt peaceful and secure. Growing drowsy, she turned out the light, snuggled down into her pillows and slept deeply.

But the peacefulness began to disintegrate into a fragmented version of her nightmare. She awoke, panting from the exertion of her dream, alternately scared and angry. *It didn't work. All that effort, and I still had the nightmare. Will it never end?* Ethan wouldn't give her any more sleeping pills, of that she was certain. But what had he told her that first day? "Fall in love or take up an exercise program." Well, falling in love took *two.* Maybe exercise was the answer.

She dragged herself out of bed, noting that it was only five o'clock, and made a pot of coffee. Showering while it perked, she tried to formulate a plan. By the time she was dressed in shorts and a shirt, she had an idea.

Last night's paper lay neatly folded on the chair. A notice for an aerobics class at the local college caught her eye. *Hmm, it's worth a try. And there's a class this morning. I wonder if I'll have time to make it?* Her sarcasm was aimed at the innocent clock that read "6:05 A.M."

Arriving a bit later, Beth found the gymnasium full of women of varying sizes and shapes. The young instructor, a picture of physical fitness, was enthusiastic and hard-driving. By the time the class was over, Beth was wringing wet and feeling righteous with accomplishment. She chose to cool down gradually by walking the gym's marked-off mile. By the time she got home she was physically tired, but a little euphoric with the increased flow of oxygen to her brain. It wasn't until the next morning that she knew the full extent of the damage to her newly used muscles.

"Oh," she groaned as she made her way to a hot shower. But she had enjoyed a deep dreamless sleep, and so the price was worth it. As it was still relatively cool when she finished her shower, she drove to the park where she and the children had gone fishing to walk the shaded trail. It wasn't marked, but she pushed herself to the limit of her sore muscles.

She continued her ritual of exercise, and gradually worked up to jogging the park trail. If nothing else, it felt good to get back into shape. She was glowing with new energy and confidence. More importantly, she was sleeping well.

I don't need Ethan or his pills, she scoffed. Beth had found a cool spot in the swing under the multitrunked hackberry tree, and was enjoying the hospitality of its shade. Locusts whirred monotonously in the noonday heat, lulling her to drowsiness. Trying to suppress a yawn, she moved into the house and crawled onto the den couch. In minutes she was asleep, her mouth curled in gentle pleasure.

She and Ethan were beside the river again. He was kissing and caressing each fingertip as he gathered her into his dream arms. As the dream moved her toward the edge of intimacy, she followed it willingly. It felt so good to be with Ethan, to have passion ruling her, to be totally female again. She looked into his eyes and knew the full extent of both their needs.

She woke to the worried pawings of Hepzibah. The cat was curled beside Beth's head, pushing on her face with soft paws.

Beth was angry at being awakened so abruptly and pushed Hepzibah away. "What's the matter with you? Can't I even nap without your bothering me?"

Hepzibah eyed her mistress, arched regally, and slipped behind the couch.

Beth couldn't decide if she was angry because she had been awakened or because she was enjoying the pleasurable dream. One thing was certain: Ethan was still too much a part of her life. He would have to go. *He's not the only man around. What do I do now?* Her glance fell on the pile of yesterday's mail, neatly stacked on the coffee table in front of her. As she riffled through the envelopes, she noticed an invitation to a principals' seminar on Friday. Dr. Kevin Todd was to be the speaker.

I haven't attended a workshop all summer, and Kevin is always a provocative speaker, she reasoned. *Who knows? Maybe I'll meet someone interesting.* No, argued her logic. *You've decided you don't need a man in your life. Go. There's always a chance you may make a contact that could lead you up the career ladder. That's a much better, more realistic reason for going. Cut out the Prince Charming syndrome. You're a modern woman—intelligent, capable of caring for yourself and your children.*

The telephone rang, ending her pep talk. "Hello."

"Hello, Beth. This is Ethan."

125

She laughed to herself at his identification, for she would have recognized that voice anywhere. "Yes?" was her cool reply.

"I was just checking to see how you are—and to apologize for the other day." He sounded concerned.

He'll never change. "I'm fine, thank you. I've taken up jogging and aerobics, so I'm sleeping like a baby. Your advice was very sound."

"I'm glad to hear that." Did she hear relief or disappointment in his voice?

"It's nice of you to call." She was about to add her goodbye when he interrupted.

"You didn't say you'd accept my apology."

On the strength of her new commitment, she said, "I accept your apology."

"Good." Now there was definitely relief in his voice. "I've found another elderly couple I'd like to interview. Would you like to go with me—Friday?"

"I'm so sorry, but I'll be attending a principals' seminar that day."

"Oh. I guess I won't see you until Sunday at church. Would you like me to pick you up? I'm sure Granny is expecting us for lunch." He sounded so sure of himself.

With the deftness of a fencer making the final thrust, she said, "I may not be in town. I'm thinking of driving up to get the children. Maybe we'd better not count on anything."

"Well . . . have a good trip." His tone had changed from confident to doubtful. "Tell the children 'hello' for me and call me if you need anything."

"I'm sure I'll be just fine now. Thank you for all your help."

"Goodbye, Beth. And the offer for help still stands."

"I know. Goodbye, Ethan."

Only the tiniest of regrets flickered in her consciousness—though she had watched a rosebud die before it bloomed fully.

Ethan's sense of professional pride was at war with his heart. *I knew I shouldn't have taken her out to the river*, he scolded himself mentally. *I knew what might happen in a romantic place like that.* He scowled at his reflection in the mirror over the low chest of drawers that stood in his bedroom. *You're crazy to take chances like that. This woman is relying on you for professional care—and what do you do?* He pointed an accusing finger at his twin. *You kiss her—again! What is the matter with you?*

He stalked away from his angry reflection, stroking his beard, a dead giveaway to his total agitation. Pacing the small living room, he continued his personal tirade. *You're acting like an adolescent. For heaven's sake, you're a grown man! And you're risking your reputation as a doctor. Why, she could even bring charges of unprofessional conduct against you!* That unsettling thought drove him into the tiny kitchen where he poured himself a tall glass of herbal tea, then distractedly set down the glass on the counter without even tasting it.

Returning to to the couch, he sat down and rubbed his tired eyes as though to regain clear thought. It eased some of his tension as he sought his own counsel. *No matter how you think you feel about her, you must maintain only a professional demeanor. To do anything else is not only unwise for you, but unsafe for her until she comes to grips with her anger. If, and I say if, you have any regard for her at all, you'll keep her needs—not yours—uppermost in your mind. You may occasionally see her, but only in order to keep touch with her progress.*

He stretched out on the couch, tired beyond belief. *Maybe the day will come . . .* But he swiftly severed the thought. In his world, this thought was not even permitted. The doctor's ultimate goal for all patients was to help them become healthy—independent of him.

Having already told Ethan she might leave town, Beth now had to consider it. It would mean spending time in an uncomfortable place. *Why didn't I just tell him no? Now I'll have to go. Of course, I could just change my mind.* She longed to go to church Sunday, but the day had developed into a ritual—sitting together, going to Granny's for lunch, and that long captive afternoon. It was relatively easy to say no to Ethan, but Granny was another problem entirely. She loved Granny, for Granny was love itself. *But can I have her company without Ethan's?* It seemed unlikely. Several plots and half-plots of how to keep going to church without hurting anyone's feelings were attempted, but the soundest was to tell Granny how she felt. *And I'd better do it today,* she thought decisively.

She dialed Granny's number. Her heart fluttered a little in anticipation of the conversation. "Hello, Granny."

"I was just thinking about you, dear. How are you—and when are my kids coming back home?"

A great sigh escaped Beth. "Granny, I have a problem."

"Shoot. I'm pretty good at problem-solving. Been doing it for so long, I guess."

"You know how much I love you, and that I want to spend time with you."

"But you feel trapped on Sundays at church and those long afternoons. Right?"

"Y-yes," Beth stammered. "But I didn't know how to tell you."

"Just like that Be honest with people, Beth, even if it sometimes means hurting their feelings. In the long run, it's easier than being deceitful. And besides, it's less time-consuming. Is Ethan completely out of your life now?"

"Yes, I'm afraid so. Granny, you're so wise. I wish I could accept life the way you do—without all the wrestling."

Granny's laugh was like tiny silver bells. "Honey,

I'm still wrestling. But it's all right; it makes my muscles stronger."

"I feel a little overtrained right now. I guess Ethan *is* out of my life. I'm not sure he was ever really in it. He used me like a convenience store. Need a family? Use Beth's. A pleasant companion for the afternoon? Ask Beth."

"It's possible," Granny said pragmatically. "But I suspect it's more likely he's just testing the water. That's a big jump for a man. Most men start with a wife first."

"Not in this day and age. Men and women combine families every day."

"But he's not a family," Granny said reasonably. "And he's been independent for a long time. Only you can decide how long to put up with his skittishness. But if anyone can gentle him, I think it's you."

Beth considered that for a second. "Maybe—if one is willing to put up with the bother. Why didn't you ever remarry, Granny?"

"Same reason. Our marriage fit us like well-worn shoes. I wasn't willing to break in a new pair."

It was Beth's turn to laugh. "Exactly!"

"'Course, one thing about being a woman is that no one considers it odd if we change our minds."

"True, but today no one considers it odd if we choose to live alone, either. Granny I've just recently discovered that I'm not married any more, and you know, it's not so bad."

"Sounds like you've reached Stage Three."

"Stage Three?"

"First there's grieving, then acceptance, then rebuilding."

"Yes, yes, that's it. The pain has subsided, and I have accepted Robert's death. I do get angry with him now and again for not being here."

"He didn't choose. It was the Lord's will."

"Don't say that to me!" The angry words shot over

129

the line before she could stop them. "I mean, surely the Lord didn't will all this unhappiness for me."

"Are you unhappy?"

"Not right at this moment. But it's been terrible at times. I couldn't want anyone to have to live through what I have."

"But we all do. Every one of us loses someone. It's just the cycle of life."

Before either of them could say something she might regret, Beth terminated the verbal tug of war. "That's true. Thanks for being so understanding, Granny."

"Beth, I think maybe I was wrong about Stage Two."

"No, you weren't. I *have* accepted Robert's death."

"Perhaps. But there's more to it than acceptance."

"I'll still work on it, Granny, honestly. And today I feel happy and confident." There was a plea hidden in her words.

"Good. Why don't you ask me to lunch next week. Maybe we could even go shopping together. I used to love shopping with my daughter. It's one of the things I miss most. I think I'll buy a pair of red shoes."

"Why red ones?"

"Because I want something cheerful, and red shoes always make me feel cheerful. You do realize I've adopted you—but not just to replace my dead daughter. You're a fine woman, Beth, and I'd have added you to my family if I'd had a dozen kids instead of just one."

Beth felt the surge of love. "Thank you, Granny. I'll call you again soon."

"Beth, come on to church. You can always sit in the choir loft. Better yet, join the choir. It would be all very natural that way."

"Hey, that's a good idea. 'Bye, Granny."

"'Bye, my love. See you soon."

With a profound sense of relief, Beth cradled the

receiver. She had smoothed out one of the largest wrinkles in her life. *At least I may finally have a good hold on my life*, and she added an afterthought. *if no One rearranges my gameboard.* And she grinned. *You know, Lord, You do have a way of doing that sort of thing. King's X? At least for a little while?* She could swear she felt Him smiling at her.

In lieu of her decision not to drive up for the children, Beth called them. They seemed so happy that she made no mention of their coming home. *Farm life provides them with so many interesting experiences*, she consoled herself as she hung up the phone.

Then another thought brought her to a new conclusion: *If I never marry again, this is how it will be when the children leave home to go to college.* Fear of the lonely years ahead crushed her, scattering all her plans, until she reasoned herself back to the present. *Take no thought for the morrow*, rushed through her brain. *No, Lord, I won't worry. I can handle each day as it comes.*

And she proceeded to plan that day. A new summer dress for the seminar tomorrow. Check to see when choir rehearsals are scheduled. Then she sang along with every song that came over the radio, for tonight would be her debut with the church choir.

Choir practice was fun and challenging, and when she got back home she was still humming the anthem they had rehearsed for so long.

Beth's life was in high gear, which made it even harder to understand why she dreamed of Ethan that night. She had no idea what she had dreamed, except that she awakened knowing that she had been with him.

Dispirited, she sipped her coffee. *How do you erase a man from your mind? Maybe I should run at night before I go to bed. That's it. Then I'll be too tired to dream of anything. But right now I'd better get myself to that seminar.*

Laying out her new dress, she smiled. "Today could be a very interesting day, cat." Hepzibah purred at Beth from "her" pillow and lifted her small pointed ears in interest. *What if I do pick up some job information today?* It was common practice to move word along that a school was looking for a new principal. It might even be in another city. *Kevin might know something. What if it means moving?* The thought was rather nicely exciting. She brushed all her speculation aside and concentrated on getting to the meeting.

Driving onto the junior college campus toward the main building, Beth felt a tug of nostalgia. The long, low white stone building with its smoked black windows was the epitome of everything up-to-date in education. For a brief moment she longed to be back in the classroom, using all that wonderful new equipment.

She followed the green-carpeted hallway to a large classroom. There was the familiar smell she always associated with school. *Maybe it's the chalk.*

A number of people had already assembled, and she greeted most of them as she made her way to an empty desk. Just as she seated herself, a tall wiry man hurried over.

"I was hoping you'd be here this morning." He took her hand in both his large ones.

"Hello, Kevin. I'm glad to see you, too."

He slid into the desk beside her. "How are your kids?"

"Fine. They're with the Martins. How are yours?"

He was gently grayed at the temples and wore a large, friendly grin. "Growing too fast. You look gorgeous, as always."

"Thank you. I bought a new dress just for the occasion." She knew she was looking her best. The summer sun had tanned her cheeks and given her a rosy glow which complemented the emerald green of her two-piece linen dress.

"How are things at school?" As the superintendent of a large district, Kevin was always on the prowl for good staff members.

"It was a hectic year," she admitted, "but a personally satisfying one."

"Too bad. I was hoping it was horrible and you might be looking for a change."

Beth shrugged her shoulders. "I'm not looking for another job, if that's what you mean. But I'm not totally disinterested." She felt a little tremble of excitement at the possibilities of starting something new.

"I have a good opening at a brand-new elementary school." His thick eyebrows rose invitingly. "The building will be completed the end of July. It has everything your little heart has ever desired —excellent staff, too."

Beth laughed. "You sound like a used-car salesman, but it does sound tempting."

"Maybe you'd better submit an application. You'd hate yourself later if you didn't." The wide smile didn't diminish, but his eyes were serious. "I'd like you to consider it. You're a crackerjack administrator. I'd love to have you in our system."

"Thank you, Kevin. I'll think very seriously about it. Hey, I think the meeting is about ready to start. Jim's been trying to get your attention."

As he walked to the front of the room, Beth thought, *You're still a charming fox. No wonder you have the best school system in the state.*

Picking up the program, she quickly scanned the day's schedule. Right after lunch Dr. Ethan Stewart was to speak on the critical health problem of unimmunized students! *But I thought he planned to interview that elderly couple!* Of course, he hadn't said how long the interview would take, nor even what time of day it had been scheduled. She glanced

133

around the large room filled with people. It shouldn't be too hard to avoid him in this crowd. He'd probably buzz in, make his pitch and leave. *You can't spend the rest of your life dodging Ethan Stewart,* she scolded herself. *Grow up.* Kevin's job offer grew more enticing by the moment.

The morning passed quickly with shop talk and valuable information being disseminated equally. She was at ease among her peers, joining the discussions and offering suggestions.

It wasn't until the group returned from lunch to the classroom that she began dreading Ethan's appearance. She took her seat again amid comments about the next poor speaker who would get the worst spot on the program. People were well-fed and relaxed, and few of them spent much time sitting, so the time right after lunch was commonly denoted as "naptime." Beth felt momentary regret that Ethan had been chosen to speak at that time and hoped his talk would be concise, sparing himself and the others some embarrassment.

In spite of all her self-admonitions, Beth was unable to stem the swirl of joy when she saw Ethan enter the room. His blue eyes gleamed with good humor, his mouth curved wide in a smile amidst his red-gold beard.

Kevin greeted him enthusiastically, then announced, "I see our next victim has arrived, ladies and gentlemen." He led Ethan to the speaker's stand as a light ripple of chuckles ruffled the crowd. When they were standing side by side, Kevin gave Ethan a brief introduction and sat down.

"Is anyone asleep yet?" Ethan's eyes roamed the audience. "At medical meetings this spot on the speakers' roster is quietly referred to as 'naptime.'" To surprised laughter and applause, Ethan added, "I see you are well aware of my position, and I of yours, so I'll be brief.

"With the recent measles outbreak in the state, we

134

are asking that you administrators tighten your requirements for immunizations before allowing students to register for school.''

As Ethan spoke, Beth tried to listen only to the information he was giving, but her eyes were drawn to his mouth. She knew that mouth and how it felt on her own. The futility of the situation was overwhelming. For whatever reason, Ethan kept her at arm's length. It was obvious to her that she couldn't avoid seeing him from time to time, and it hurt each time they met.

If I can get away from him, I'll stop dreaming about him. I'm not running away, I'm doing the most logical thing. I'll send in an application for that job. Maybe I'll even go back to school and get my doctorate.

Having made a decision it was easier to listen impartially to the rest of Ethan's speech. She had a life to live and it was time for her to get on with it.

Ethan finished his presentation and thanked the audience for its attention.

Beth was watching him as he gathered up his brief notes. He stopped and looked at her squarely, a wistful smile playing across his lips. For a moment she thought he was going to come back and sit with her, but he turned and walked through the door—and out of her life.

CHAPTER 8

"Now, WHERE DID I PUT THAT THING ?" Beth dug through her personal files, looking for the information she needed to finish her application. "It's been so long since I had to prove I've been to school. I know it, and they know it, or I wouldn't be a principal in the first place!"

She clenched her teeth as she began the tedious task of filling in the multitude of facts required of her. "Why in the world would they want to know that?" Dutifully she filled in the blank. "One of the first things I'm going to do if I ever become a superintendent is to revise these dumb application forms."

It took almost an hour to finish the job and add her certifications from the state to the bulging envelope, but she was cheerful as she licked the stamp to send it on its way.

She had excellent credentials, and she knew she had more than a good chance of securing the position.

What if I get the job? What would I do with the house? Sell? Rent? I wonder what kind of housing is available there? A thousand details suddenly sprang to mind when she considered the reality of moving. Uppermost was how the children might take it. *Everyone moves sometime. They'll adjust.* But deep in her heart she knew it would be a wrenching experience for them, for they had lived their entire lives in this place.

Maybe I'd better just cross one bridge at a time, she thought. *I don't even have the job yet.* But her heart was pounding as she slipped the letter into the mailbox, knowing that the outcome could completely change all their lives in the blink of an eye. *Lord, bless this endeavor and show me by the answer what I'm to do with my life. I don't know if I'm supposed to move or not. Show me,* Beth prayed as she walked back into the house from the mailbox.

Hepzibah, standing patiently by her bowl, was waiting for Beth to notice that she had no milk. She looked balefully at her mistress, as if to say, "How could you forget one of the most important matters of the day?"

"I'm sorry, cat. I'm discombobulated today. You know," she said, "mixed up, forgetful." Stroking the cat as she poured the milk, Beth realized that there was more truth in that statement than she cared to admit.

Was she letting Ethan run her out of town? Or was she really taking charge of her life and making a qualified career decision? *Only the Lord knows for sure, and He hasn't let me in on it yet,* she decided, and grabbed up her workout clothes on her way out the door to the gym.

The routines were easier now for her, and she put everything she had into them—stretching and moving hard. She felt free as she did the aerobic exercises, newly acquainted with her body's ability to move quickly and gracefully. *I feel like the Tin Man after Dorothy oiled him,* and she smiled as she thought of the time-honored *Oz* she had read so many times to her children.

On the way home she impulsively stopped by Granny's.

"I didn't know if I'd find you home or not," she said to Granny's perpetually smiling face as she opened the door.

"You lucked out! My Bunko Club meeting was postponed. Millie has the flu. Come on in and have something to drink. My goodness, Beth, you look wonderful. What have you been up to?"

Beth followed her into the shining kitchen and accepted a tall glass of minted lemonade. "I've just come from my exercise class." She took a deep swallow. "I never knew how good I could feel until I started this class. And," she added smugly, "I'm sleeping like a baby."

"Why wouldn't you? A person your age *should* sleep well at night." Granny sat at the table with her.

"I never told you before, but I've had trouble with terrible nightmares," Beth said quietly. "That was how I met Ethan. I went to his office to get some help."

"He must have had the answer. You look terrific."

"He did, and he didn't," she admitted. Beth shared the entire story with Granny.

Granny sat quietly for a while, thinking. "Fall in love or take up exercise, huh? That's just like a man, although I guess he *could* be right. I think you should have talked to your pastor myself."

"Why?"

"Because it was after Robert's death that you began to have the nightmares. I think it was your heart, not your head, that needed fixing."

Beth took another sip of her lemonade, taking time to formulate her answer and deal with the tiniest flicker of anger. "Granny, why do you think I've had these nightmares?"

"As I told you before, I don't think you've worked your way through Stage Two of your grief." Granny took off her old-fashioned glasses and polished them needlessly. "I don't think you've ever gotten being mad at Robert for dying and leaving you and the kids. Maybe you're even still mad at God."

"I may be mad at Robert, but it's a sin to be mad at *God*. I don't want to talk about it, anyway, because now I have everything under control." She told Granny about the job offer.

"I'm afraid that by the time you leave here, you'll be sorry that you stopped by, Beth dear, but I've always felt it best to speak my mind." Granny didn't flinch from her self-appointed job as Speaker of the Truth. "You're still mad because of Robert's death, and you're running away from Ethan. Until you face both these problems and solve them, you're not going to be happy anywhere."

Beth tried hard not to let Granny see her mounting anger. Carefully she chose her next words. "I know you're just trying to help, Granny, but I think I know what I'm doing—what's best for me and my children. Because I love you, I don't want to talk about it anymore. I'll think about what you've said, but I think you're wrong. I've prayed about the job, and I'll wait to see what the Lord wants me to do about it."

Granny reached across the table to take Beth's hand in her own. "I'm glad you've talked to Him about it. I know He'll be your best source of help. And," she said impishly, "I'll try to keep my nose out of your business unless you ask me for help, too."

"Who knows, Granny? You may be right. Right now, though, I think I'd better start for home." She rose and made her way to the door. As she walked out into the hot summer air, she said casually, "I'm seriously thinking about having the children come back home. I miss them more than I even allow myself to think about."

"Good! I miss them, too. Call me when they get back and we'll have another ice cream party. Want to go shopping tomorrow afternoon?"

"Hmm, sounds like fun. About two?"

"Pick me up. I'll be ready."

Driving home, Beth couldn't keep Granny's words from echoing in her ears. *Maybe she's right. Am I still angry? I don't think I am. There's too much good happening in my life now for me to dwell on the past. I have let go. I live only for today. And today is the day I'm going to arrange to have the children come home.*

Beth called and spoke with them, missing them even more as she heard their sweet voices, then made arrangements with the Martins for their trip home, and hung up the phone, almost counting the hours until the arrival time the next day. *I'll still have time to go shopping with Granny. We'll just have to make it in the morning, rather than the afternoon.*

She called Granny early the next day and explained the change in plans.

"I'd love to, Beth, but I was going to call you and let you know I I couldn't make it, anyway. Let's plan to do it next week. And after the children are resettled, we'll have that party."

Granny didn't sound like herself. Beth waited for her to explain what was going on, but refrained. After Granny had promised to stay out of her business, she didn't feel free to interfere in hers. "All right. I'll call you again soon."

She met the noon plane with her heart almost bursting with excitement. The children clambered off the plane and into her waiting arms with a thousand kisses and at least that many questions. The conversation didn't lag for a second during the first few hours they were together. There was too much news and too many events to share.

It was close to midnight when she had them

snuggled into their beds, and was about to ready herself for her own bed when the phone rang.

"Beth." Ethan's voice sounded tense.

As soon as she heard it, she was tempted to cut the conversation as short as humanly possible. "Yes, Ethan?" *How dare he think he could call her so late at night!*

"I have admitted Granny to the hospital. Could you come right away?"

"What happened? Is she all right?" Beth tried to still the sudden sense of foreboding.

"Her condition is stable. About two hours ago she called me, asking me to come for her. She's had a coronary and is in the intensive care unit. She's asking for you."

"I'll be there as quickly as I can after I call my neighbor to stay with the children. Ethan, is she going to make it?"

"I can't promise anything. The fact that she has lived this long is a good sign. But the first seventy-two hours are the critical ones. If she doesn't have another attack, she has a good chance."

Beth prayed her way to the hospital. *Please, God, don't let her die. Don't let her suffer. Lord, be merciful to this gentle soul. Don't take her from us. We need her so much.*

Tears slipped out of the corner of her eyes and traced a path down her shirt front. The fervent pleas continued on her trip through the front doors to the special section reserved for critical care patients. The nurse asked Beth to wait in the small room beside the unit until Ethan could come out and speak to her. An eternity passed before he appeared, and Beth ran into his arms in gratitude.

His face was strained and a little pale, but he attempted to reassure her. "She's a bit dopey from the drugs, but you can go in and see her for five minutes. It will do her good to know you're here."

141

It seemed natural to be standing in the hallway with Beth in his arms, carefully listening to his every word.

"It's imperative that she not sense any fear, so wipe that grim look off your face, and be matter-of-fact about her recovery. She must feel nothing but a positive outlook from you."

Beth moved out of his arms, and dried her eyes. Her smile was a little damp, but it was a smile. "There, is that better?"

"Fine. Five minutes. I'll talk with you when you come back out. Come down to my office and we'll have a cup of coffee."

Beth didn't question any of his orders. This was his world, and, here he was the ultimate authority. Meekly she pushed through the double doors that led to a brightly lit circular room with a nursing station in the center. She had tried to be very quiet, but there was constant activity here as the nurses cared for these special patients. There were no private cubicles, only screens for use during treatment or examination. The patients' beds were arranged around the room, in full view of the nurses, like the beds at a children's camp.

As Beth approached Granny's bed, she was alarmed by all the paraphernalia above the white head and at her side. All kinds of lights and equipment blinked and whirred. It was an alien world, running on its own time and by its own rules.

"Granny?" Beth was afraid to touch her, for there were many tubes running in and out of her body, like shields that stood between them. She stepped closer to the bed, leaning down to see if Granny had heard her.

"Granny," she whispered again. "I'm here. You gave us quite a fright, but I can see you are getting super care. I brought the children home. As soon as you're moved to a regular room, I'll bring them to see you. It shouldn't be long. You're a fighter."

Granny's eyes were closed in drug-induced rest, but Beth thought she saw the merest nod of her head. She looked so tiny and defenseless lying there. Her usually neat hair was a little disheveled, but still in place. The hospital gown was the standard tiny-print affair, but it inadequately hid the small body with the tubes marching in and out. Beth had an impulse to knock away all the tubes and make Granny more comfortable in her own bed, but reason prevailed, and she reluctantly acknowledged that these very tubes were probably helping to keep Granny alive. Beth caught the gesture of a nurse and knew she had to leave. "Granny, I love you, and I'll see you again soon." The tears she had held back began to flow freely as she left the room and started for Ethan's office.

They were spent by the time she reached his door and knocked.

"Come in." Ethan was leaning back in his desk chair with his feet propped on his desk. He looked dreadfully tired, and his white smock was stained with something dark. "Sit down." His everything-will-be-all-right façade was gone.

Beth sat and accepted the cup of coffee he offered her, realizing that she, too, was bone-weary. "Ethan, she looks so awful. Do you really think she has a chance?"

Ethan's eyes were kind. "I'm only a man, Beth. At best, all I have is the finest equipment the medical world has to offer. But sometimes that isn't enough. Right now, it is literally up to the Lord."

"But what does the Lord want? She just can't die, Ethan. She has so much left to do. So many people depending on her." Fear crept in, filling her.

"And you and I are two of those who depend on her most." He took his feet off the desk and leaned forward across it, reaching for her with his words. "As a doctor, I can't bear to lose any patient. When it's someone I love as much as I love Granny, there is no way to measure the guilt.''

Beth struggled for the right words, twisting her hands as she brought her thoughts to her lips. ''Ethan, I've spent long hours thinking about this. I used to lie in bed at night after Robert died, trying to decide how I felt about it.'' Tears formed on her long lashes, and spilled into her words. ''I would rather have him, and Granny, dead than have them survive only as vegetables. I can't stand the thought of them lying there, having to be cared for, kept alive past their time. I think God has blessed us with wonderful doctors and medical miracles, but there is a time to use them and a time to let go.''

Ethan answered softly. ''Those are the times I pray for strength and wisdom . . . and for the Lord's mercy.''

Beth was certain that she had never loved any man more than she loved Ethan at this moment. He was the essence of everything manly and good. All the qualities of his strength shone through those blue eyes and held her tightly. She wanted to hide in his arms as she had wanted to in his office that first day, to feel his heart beating strongly against hers. But a stupid desk stood between them, blocking her way. He made no move to rise and come to her, but sat there, comforting her long distance, doctor to patient, not man to woman. It was one of her darkest moments and she had no emotional reserves to deal with it.

''I need to go home now and get some things.'' She stood a bit shakily, and moved to the door. ''I'll be back as soon as I have things lined up at home. Call me immediately if there's any change.''

''I will. You should get some rest. Granny will likely sleep through the night. You can come back first thing in the morning.''

''I'll bet you say that to the families of all your patients,'' she smiled tiredly. ''You're probably right, but I doubt if many of them take your advice. We're afraid our loved ones might die without us, and we'll suffer terrible guilt along with the grief." She left his office and stumbled down the corridor. She had given voice to the feelings that still lived deep within her.

Robert had died alone. She didn't even know he was dead until the policeman arrived at the door. Now she drove automatically, reliving the horror of that day. Had Robert been frightened, or was he unconscious, as Granny seemed to be? When Beth had been allowed to see him, he was lying quiet and still in a hospital bed, his eyes closed eternally. It wasn't her Robert she had seen. It was a parody of him, inanimate and unfamiliar. She had sent him off to work that morning, and that was the last time she ever saw him alive. He had gone away and left her. Not only that—he had done it by himself. She had no chance to comfort or encourage him. His death was a totally private act, and she was angry at him for not allowing her to share it as they had shared so many other events.

This time Beth had been forewarned, and she was determined that if Granny had to die, she wouldn't die by herself. Beth hurriedly gathered her things together and headed back to the hospital to sit nearby in the small waiting room. The neighbor agreed to care for the children until she returned.

Her vigil was long as Granny and Ethan fought for Granny's life. The short visiting period she was allowed at intervals throughout the day did nothing to lift her spirits. But as the last of the critical seventy-two-hour period came to a close, Granny seemed to rally. For the first time Beth began to feel hopeful that her incessant prayers for Granny's life had been answered.

She was sitting in the waiting room drinking coffee when Ethan appeared.

"Granny is asking for you." His face masked his

145

emotion as he led her to the door of the intensive care unit.

Swiftly she moved to Granny's bedside. "Yes, Granny, I'm here." She took the fragile hand offered to her.

Granny's face had an ethereal translucence and her eyes seemed to be fixed on another plane—one she alone could see. Her smile was one of eager assent. Beth recognized a gentle excitement that seemed to energize the weak body.

"Granny, I'm here," Beth said again.

"It's so beautiful, Beth." Her smile illuminated her pale face. "And, Beth, it's all right if you fight with him." And she closed her eyes to slip away from them into a place she seemed to choose, beyond the reach of human hands and instruments.

Beth felt Ethan behind her and turned around to walk into his arms. She couldn't cry, for Granny had seemed so happy that she felt only envy, not sorrow, at her death. The tears would come later, but for now she was content to stay in the circle of Ethan's arms. What had Granny meant? Who was it all right to fight with? Ethan? That was the only logical answer. Granny was sanctioning their relationship. Had Ethan heard her? He must have, or he would not have taken her in his arms.

He led her from the room and they walked to his office. "It's all right to cry." His face was composed and thoughtful.

"I know, but I don't feel like crying right now. It's the first time I've ever seen anyone die, and it was so peaceful." She struggled with the words to describe her feelings. "I felt almost envious of her. She knew something I didn't, and she wasn't afraid at all. In fact, she seemed anxious to hurry everything."

He nodded. "I've seen this before. As Christians we teach that heaven is our goal, but it's hard for us to imagine how really wonderful it is, looking from this side."

"I just can't get over how peaceful it was—not at all what I expected. I thought she'd fight right to the end." Beth shook her head helplessly.

"There's a time to fight and a time to let go."

"I guess the trick is to know when to do which."

"I'll take care of the arrangements. I know Granny left everything in an orderly state. Why don't you go home and tell your children."

"Yes, I need to do that . . . Ethan, I feel so strange. I was prepared to fend death off with my bare hands for her, and now I'm standing here—smiling."

"I know, I feel the same way. And I don't feel a trace of guilt." Ethan's face was stretched in a large grin. "I wish it could be this way every time." He sobered. "It isn't always—especially in the case of a child or someone who needs more time."

"I'm going to go now. Suddenly I'm very tired. Please call when you know the details. Goodbye, Ethan."

On the way home she tried to think of the best way to share her experience with the children. How could they possibly understand something she was having trouble understanding for herself? *Tell me what to say, Lord*, she prayed. And then there was Granny's admonition, which kept running through her head. *It's all right if you fight with him*. Fight—with whom? Granny had to mean Ethan. There just wasn't any other explanation.

Beth pulled into the driveway and walked next door to get the children. She evaded all questions until they could be alone.

Sean was the most persistent in his questioning, but she led them into the living room, seating them both in front of her.

"I just came from the hospital where I've had a most extraordinary experience." Both children

147

watched her carefully, sensing the importance of her words. "We all loved Granny so much that none of us wanted to give her up. But I was with Granny when she died, and it was a very happy time. She was anxious to go to live with Jesus—just as you were eager to make the plane trip to see your grandparents—and she smiled all the time she was leaving."

"Are Granny and Dad in the same place? Will they know each other?" Sean asked.

"Yes, I think they are, and I think they will know each other. Sean, the Lord doesn't tell us all the facts about heaven. He usually explains things in a story. I've never been to the moon, and so it's hard for me to know exactly what the astronauts mean when they talk about what they saw. But I get the general idea. God said heaven was going to be a very happy place—a place where we would be with Him all the time. There's no sickness there, nor any of the other bad things we know here on earth."

"You mean I won't get skinned knees and have to wear a bandage?" Cally's eyes were wide with wonder, for she was commonly referred to around their house as the "Band-aid kid."

"That's right. Everyone will have a perfect body and will be happy all the time."

"What will we do in heaven? My friend said we'd all have harps to play, and wings. I don't think I could ever get used to wearing those things!"

Beth laughed. "I think your friend is mistaken. Long ago, artists who painted pictures of angels used wings as a symbol that angels could move around freely to do God's work. But there are really only two things I want you to remember about heaven. It will be perfect—and we will be with God. We won't know for sure about all the other things until we get there."

"That'll be a long time for me," Cally said confidently.

"I hope so," Beth said, rejecting any other ideas.

"Did you already bury Granny?" Apparently Sean could vaguely remember his father's funeral.

"Not yet, honey. Would you and Cally like to go to the service?"

Both nodded solemnly.

"Ethan will call and let us know when it's going to be." Beth crinkled her forehead thoughtfully. "We really need to go to Granny's first, though, and make sure everything is neat. I imagine that's where everyone will gather. Do you want to go with me?"

Strangely subdued, the children nestled close to her and Beth found herself in the familiar role of comforter. At the moment, however, she wanted nothing more than to be comforted.

It seemed too quiet with no Granny to greet them with a cheery hello. The children were still as mice. Everything was tidy except for a few dishes in the sink and Granny's unmade bed.

The tears began to flow as Beth made it. The intimacy of Granny's bedroom made her realize that Granny would never be with them again, and all her weeping couldn't change that fact. She didn't try to hide her tears from the children, and when they came in to help, she gathered them into her arms and they shared their grief.

"I keep thinking Granny will come in any minute with a big plate of cookies," Sean said.

"Or to ask us to play 'Go Fishin','" added Cally with a sigh.

They finished their tasks and locked up the house. Beth had the undeniable feeling that an important chapter of her life was ending.

On the day of the funeral Ethan was kind and attentive, acting as the official head of the family, for Granny had no close relatives.

Respecting Granny's often-stated wishes, the order

of the funeral service was reversed. The committal of the body was first; then, a memorial service at the church. "Seeing someone planted in the ground is such a depressing sight, don't you think? I don't want to be remembered that way. I want my friends to hear the minister talk about all the good things that are happening right that moment. I want things to end on a happy note." And Ethan respected her request.

It was a far better way, Beth realized. The church service was upbeat and hopeful, centering on the resurrection and reminding them all of the Lord's promise that all believers would someday be with Him in paradise.

Spending so much time with Ethan as a pseudofamily was disconcerting for Beth. He was attentive, but scrupulously careful to avoid all appearances of being more than a dear friend of the family. Granny had said it was all right to fight with him, but there was never any reason to during their days together. She longed for closeness, for physical comfort; however, Ethan remained impeccably polite and distant, only putting his arm around her as Granny's casket was lowered into the earth.

Beth was exhausted at night, and slept restlessly. The nightmare did not recur. But she wrestled with disembodied problems that had to be resolved, and awakened each morning, spent and disspirited.

The day after the funeral Beth drove by the house. It looked deserted and forlorn. Setting the sprinklers to water the grass and flowers Granny loved so, Beth went inside to water the other plants.

It was a grand old house, large and cheerful, with many windows to let in the sun. There were several bedrooms in addition to the parlor, the kitchen, the dining room and the huge screened-in back porch. She wandered through the rooms, imagining Granny here as a bride, and later, as a young mother.

This house is meant for laughter and children, she

thought. Surely it must have been lonely for Granny at times. Yet, she had never complained. The Sunday dinners Beth had come to dread were probably the highlight of the week for Granny. *And I made such a fuss about those Sunday afternoons!* Guilt gave her a painful nudge, and she clenched her teeth. *Why do I always learn everything too late?*

Angrily she wished Granny back into her life so she could make up for the loneliness she might have caused. But of course no one answered her summons. She walked out of the house, regret her companion, knowing full well that this was a common reaction among bereaved people.

It was certainly one of her most consistent feelings after Robert's death. Knowing that it was normal didn't make it any less real or easier to deal with, however.

She checked the mailbox before she went inside her own home and found the usual junk mail. But one letter on the bottom caught her immediate attention. It was from Kevin's office. Quickly she slit the envelope and withdrew the single page.

"Dear Beth," it read. "I was very pleased to get your application. It has been processed with the others and I have the happy privilege of informing you that here are now only two contenders for the spot. Will you be able to come in for an official interview? Please call my office and set up an appointment convenient for both of us. Regards, Kevin."

Beth smiled broadly, pleased that she was seriously being considered. Her first impulse was to share her good news with the children. But there was no point in telling them anything until she knew for sure.

Checking her calendar, she called Kevin's office and made her appointment for the following week. She had just replaced the receiver when the phone rang.

"Hello."

"Hi, Beth, this is Ethan."

Her heart had stopped doing flip-flops when she heard his voice, but its deep timbre still gave her pleasure. "Yes, what can I do for you?"

"Granny's lawyer called me this morning. He wants us to be there for the reading of her will tomorrow morning."

"Whatever for? Could she have left something to the children?"

"It's also possible she left something to you." He sounded very matter-of-fact.

"What time and where?"

"Ten o'clock. Shall I come for you?"

Beth disliked the idea, but made a swift decision. Maybe it would be easier to lean on Ethan just once more. "Yes."

He seemed pleased, though Beth viewed it only as another one of his acts of charity. He'd had ample opportunity in the past week to further their relationship, had he so desired—and he had done nothing more than could be expected of any good counselor, any friend.

She dressed carefully in a summer print dress that draped her body softly and was ready when the doorbell rang.

Ethan stood there on the porch, looking a little like an uncertain suitor. She hadn't expected that. It was so confusing. "Hello. Are you ready to go?"

"Yes." She turned and locked the door behind her and got into Ethan's car.

Beth's hands were clasped in a tight ball in her lap. "I don't want to make this trip, Ethan. It just doesn't seem right to be present at the division of her property."

"I know. I feel that way, too." He glanced at her quickly. "Since we have been requested to be there, it is obvious she has left something to us." His eyes went back to the road.

"Or to the children. I think she might have done that for them." A sigh accompanied the frown on her face. "Ethan, I feel like a vulture waiting for a good meal. I don't want anything of Granny's, yet just going there tells everyone that I expect something." Her mouth was set in a tight line of distaste.

"Did you actively campaign to get something out of Granny?"

"Certainly not! The thought never crossed my mind! I loved her for herself!"

"Then quit feeling guilty. You have been requested to be there. So have I. We're on our way to find out what Granny wanted done with her worldly goods." A grin lit his face. "Knowing Granny, it might turn out to be a very interesting day. She was something." His voice trembled slightly. "I miss her so much."

Beth reached out and patted his shoulder gently. "I know. So do I. Her death has torn a big hole in my life." She removed her hand, careful not to let her feelings be any more than sympathetic. She was glad when the office building came into sight. "I hope this is mercifully short."

"I'm sure it will be. Granny never liked to drag her feet about anything."

The truth of his statement cheered them both as they entered the building.

CHAPTER 9

BETH AND ETHAN WERE USHERED into Solomon Lake's well-appointed office and seated in richly upholstered wing chairs.

Only moments later Solomon came bustling in, carrying a sheaf of papers. His reputation matched that of his namesake. He was known as a man who could produce a solution to almost every problem, even at the relatively young age of thirty-five. Of average height, with coal-black hair lightly salted at the temples, his youthful face belied his expertise in his field.

He extended his hand to Beth and then to Ethan, greeting them in a friendly, businesslike manner, and then seated himself behind his antique desk. "I'm glad you could both come on such short notice."

"Will the others be here, too?" asked Ethan.

"There are no others, Dr. Stewart. Mrs. Reed had only a distant cousin on her mother's side, and he is not included in the will." He smoothed out the papers in front of him. "Are we ready to begin?"

"I suppose so," Beth said as Ethan nodded his assent.

Solomon read the standard introduction that verified the legality of the document for the disposition of Emma Lambert Reed's worldly goods. It was the next part of the will that caused Beth and Ethan to exchange startled looks.

"My most important goal during my earthly life has been to share my faith in Jesus as my Savior," he read. "I want this last chance to speak to others around me of the fact that it was my most important goal in life, and even beyond. God is good and He loves us all."

Solomon paused to interject a thought. "This, of course, is not the usual will. Mrs. Reed chose to do one more thing out of the ordinary. The rest of the will is written out, at my insistence, but I agreed to a rather unorthodox procedure."

He reached into the top right-hand drawer and took out a small cassette player. There was a tape already inserted and he pushed the button and sat back in his chair to listen with them.

Beth's face was a study in astonishment as Granny's sweet voice, clear and firm, spoke to them. "I'm so glad Ethan introduced me to this machine. It has been a pleasure to use on so many occasions. Now I want to use it for something I think is most important. I want to tell you exactly how I want my estate handled. I don't own a lot of earthly possessions, just things I thought I needed to be comfortable. Everything else I gave away a long time ago. But I did have some of the dearest people in the world to love and be loved by.

"Ethan, I want to speak to you first."

Automatically Beth glanced toward Ethan's grave face as Granny's voice continued.

"I'm sure it was you who valiantly fought the battle for my earthly life, and I want to thank you for that and all the loving times you provided me. Now don't you feel guilty that you lost the battle. I won the war." A smile crept into Ethan's misty eyes. "I already know that where I'm going is much to be preferred. This old life cannot compare to the new.

"Now, Beth, it's your turn."

Full-blossomed tears rolled down her cheeks as Beth heard Granny speak her name.

"You've brought so much happiness into my life with your wonderful family. You and Sean and Cally added immeasurably to the joy of my days. And I'm sorry that I made a promise to you a long time ago not to speak to Ethan about his nonsense." Beth turned absolutely scarlet and looked at the floor.

"It's because you two can't seem to figure out what's going on that I decided to dispose of my worldly goods in this way. You are to inherit my property equally—Mr. Lake will give you all the details. But you may not sell any of it for a period of five years. If you can't get together by then, you should sell everything and part ways. In the meantime, I don't want the house unoccupied. Now don't get excited! I want Ethan to move into it and live there. Beth, I want you to clean it and keep things running smoothly. It may be inconvenient. If so, I'm sorry, but this is the way I want it. You'll have to decide who is to do what and when, but I want the property maintained by both of you during that five-year period."

By this time Ethan and Beth were in a state of shock. They weren't so naïve as to believe they would have been left out of the will entirely, but they were totally unprepared for the enormity of her plan.

"Now don't just dismiss the idea as the scheme of an eccentric old lady. You're fine people, both of you, and I'd like to see you make a go of it as a family. This

156

is the only way I could think to make you listen to each other. That's the reason I had Mr. Lake draw up a new will. If I say too much more, I might spoil the surprises you will discover as you spend time together. Goodbye and work hard to love and accept each other.''

Solomon flipped the cassette off and waited for the two stunned people in his office to compose themselves. They stared at him in disbelief.

"Yes, this will is perfectly legal," he anticipated their first question. "Inconvenient, but legal and binding. I have an inventory of her property if you care to see it."

There was a white line etched around Ethan's firmly closed mouth. "Whatever made Granny think this was a good idea?"

"I agree with you, Dr. Stewart, but this is the way she wanted it and no amount of discussion could dissuade her."

Beth's blush had faded to pallor. "Ethan, if I'd had any idea what she was planning, I'd have spoken to her. I'm embarrassed that you are put in this position. I'm embarrassed for myself, too."

Ethan's shock visibly dissipated, and he began to smile broadly. "Well, at least we know exactly what she expects of us."

"I don't find any of this amusing at all. I'm considering a new job in another school district, and this will change all my plans."

"Where is this new job?" Ethan was looking steadily at her ashen face.

"Not in this town, and—and I don't feel I need to defend myself to you."

Solomon smiled. "This is exactly what I told Granny would happen if she insisted on going through with her plans. I guess you've heard the story about the two mules that were put in a double harness. It took them awhile to learn to work together and not just pull in opposite directions. It'll work out, if you just give it time. If you have any more questions you'd like to ask, you have only to call. I'll see that both of you receive copies of the will." He was still smiling broadly.

Beth rose, sighing, and offered her hand to Solomon. "You're going to need all that wisdom to help us through this one."

"No, ma'am," he corrected her. "*You're* going to need it." He shook hands with Ethan and walked them to the door. "Let me know if the water gets too deep."

They were more than halfway home before Ethan finally broke the thoughtful silence between them. "Beth, if I'd had any idea that she was going to do this, I would have stopped her. It's not fair to put you in this awkward position. In spite of Granny's good intentions, she was wrong this time. We have been friends, and we will always remain friends. If you decide to take this new job, we'll work out something about your part of the will. This is between you and me now. Granny has nothing to do with it." His face was grim in the lights of the oncoming traffic. "I've seen too many people's lives ruined by death-bed promises, and I won't have yours added to the list."

"But this wasn't a death-bed wish—this was her will," Beth argued.

"It's essentially the same thing. Emotional blackmail."

Beth was shocked. "Ethan! How can you say such a thing. I don't care about Granny's property, but I do think we ought to respect her wishes."

"Even if it ruins all your plans?"

Beth hesitated. "My plans are not official yet. I may not even get the job." Her reply was coolly detached. Ethan had stated his preference about their relationship—and she had heard it—loud and clear. He wanted to be her friend, her counselor, her

158

doctor—nothing more. Impulsively she promised herself, *If I get that job, I'm going to pack and get out of here. Ethan's right. It wasn't fair of Granny to use her will like a carrot in front of a donkey. She can't make him love me.* The more she thought about it, the madder it made her.

When Ethan stopped his car in front of her house, she didn't even wait for him to open her door, but hopped out and dismissed him curtly. "Thanks for the ride. And the advice. I think you may be right about Granny's will." And she walked away without waiting for him to escort her to the door.

Inside, the house was blessedly quiet. With the children visiting next door, there was time to think through all the things that had so recently rocked her world. She retreated into the sanctuary of her bedroom and lay down on her bed. Hepzibah was quick to join her, purring with pleasure at Beth's return.

"I don't have time for you right now, Hepzibah." The cat ignored the rebuff, and, still purring, curled herself into a furry ball beside Beth. "I must get that job. It's driving me crazy to see Ethan, knowing all he wants from me is friendship." A tear escaped from the corner of her eye and rolled down to the pillow with a plop. "I'm living on a dead-end street. No Ethan, no Granny." She was afraid to voice the feeling that maybe God had turned a deaf ear to all her pleas, too. That was too terrifying to contemplate.

Granny's request that Beth and Ethan take care of her house was also overwhelming. They would be thrown together constantly. *I'm back to those long Sunday afternoons, except that they might last for five years.* Another gargantuan tear joined the first. Others followed in rapid succession until she fell asleep . . .

She was sitting in a classroom, behind a student's desk. Ethan was seated behind her, and they were preparing to take a test. At the front of the room was the teacher. It was Granny, and she was smiling because she knew the test was very difficult and only she knew all the answers. Ethan kept coaching Beth, whispering the answers, until Granny's voice chastized her severely. "Go to the principal's office. You're supposed to know the answers already, young lady." Shame overwhelmed her and she slunk out of the room, angry because Ethan had caused her so much trouble.

Of course she knew how to find the principal's office, but the hallway led her through a maze of corridors, going nowhere. She *must* find the principal. She tried to open one of the doors in the hallway to ask for help, but they were all locked. No one would help her and when, in her despair, she called aloud, she woke herself.

Struggling to a sitting position, she tried to clear her head of her dream. *Am I going mad?* In a hazy panic she pulled on her jogging togs and hurried outside. *Fresh air and exercise are what I need. I haven't kept up my running, and that's why I'm having bad dreams again. Run, Beth, run!*

The administration building was modern and sleek, a fitting work environment for Dr. Kevin Todd. Beth noted that everything was in keeping with his concepts of education. He practiced what he preached.

She gave her name to his secretary and sat down to wait her turn. A dark-haired man was sitting across from her. *I wonder if he's my competition.*

"Mrs. Martin, Dr. Todd will see you now." Beth fought the tiny butterflies fluttering in her stomach. So much was riding on this interview. Before, it was only a pleasant option. Now she needed that job. She smoothed down the skirt of her crisp navy blue suit and walked with more confidence than she felt toward her appointment with her future. *Please, God, let me get this job.*

Kevin rose from his desk to greet her. "Good

morning, Beth. I'd like you to meet the assistant superintendent, Roger Dale.''

Kevin motioned her to a chair and she sat down gratefully. ''I asked Roger if I could sit in on this interview, though it is not our usual procedure. He's pretty much in charge of hiring. But the vacancy we are trying to fill will require an extraordinary administrator. The board has indulged me once again and we are going to do some revolutionary things in this new school. Roger, why don't you fill her in?''

Dr. Dale explained the avant-garde program that he and Kevin were planning and the qualities required for the administrator. ''How do you feel about this program, Mrs. Martin? Do you think it is a plausible one?''

Beth's eyes were shining with excitement. ''Not only do I think it will work, I think it's the way education *must* go in order to meet the needs of the future! It's so revolutionary that we may have a hard time selling it to the parents, but with proper P.R., I know it can be sold. I'd love the opportunity to be in on this one!'' She felt energized, exhilarated.

For over an hour the three of them discussed Beth's qualifications and the specific needs of the program. She was so involved in the discussion that she was surprised when Kevin began to wind things down.

''I think we have a good grasp of your ideas now, Beth. You have some sound ones, but in all fairness, we must interview our other applicant.'' He rose in a gesture of dismissal.

A stab of disappointment slashed Beth. She felt that she had been allowed into a candy store only to be told that she would have to wait to actually taste the chocolates. ''Yes, of course.'' She left the room, both elated and disappointed with Kevin's promise to call her tomorrow with his decision.

She couldn't help speculating on what a yes might mean to her little family. On the way home, she sorted

161

through the possibilities. Sell the house, or rent it. Pay for a move. Granny's house? Hire someone to clean it. Change schools for both children.

That would be a major adjustment. Cally loved the day care center, and Sean was so excited with the teacher he had already been assigned for the next year.

Find a new dentist. A pharmacy. A new doctor. No more Ethan to see and not be able to reach. *I'm not running away*, she argued. *I'm taking care of myself. I wonder if all my bad dreams, and the romantic ones involving Ethan will go away now*.

As she drove through the town she loved, the happy years spent there passed in review outside the windshield.

Here, she and Robert had come as newlyweds and had purchased their first modest home. In this place, their bright hopes yet untarnished, they had lived and loved and created two beautiful babies. Here, too, Robert had gone away and left them to wrestle the twin demons of loneliness and change. And then Ethan had entered her life, challenging her faith and stirring feelings she had thought were buried with Robert.

Her faith had been buffeted and battered through all of this. There seemed to be nothing but a steady stream of nos in answer to her prayers. Now trouble tugged at her like an undertow, threatening to submerge her.

Thinking of Granny reminded Beth that she needed to go by the house and keep her part of the bargain. She pulled into the driveway and hurried inside to change her clothes. Retrieving the children from the new babysitter next door, she loaded them into the car, despite their protests.

"I don't like going over there anymore, now that Granny's not home." Sean was adamant. "I don't like going into an empty house. It's spooky." Cally nodded in agreement. "Besides, it's all locked."

"No, it's not." Beth handed him the key that had been taped to the bottom of the will. "You may open the door for me."

When they arrived, Sean manfully fitted the key in the lock and they entered where they didn't wish to be.

Beth's eyes opened wide, for Ethan had obviously already moved into the house. "I didn't think about that," she muttered under her breath. To the children, she spoke brightly. "You guys don't bother anything of Ethan's. Cally, you dust the parlor. Sean, you can sweep off the back porch. I'll run the vacuum."

It is spooky. She found it even more disconcerting when she began to clean the back bedroom that Ethan had taken for his own. She made his bed and dusted around his personal things in the room. Hanging his clothes and cleaning his bathroom was almost an ordeal. She tried not to notice the scent of his aftershave lotion, for it brought him right into the room with her. *This is not going to work. I'll have to hire someone to do this.* The sound of his voice behind her startled her so that she dropped the cleaning cloth in her hand. "Oh!" she gasped. "You scared me half to death!"

"I'm sorry. I just came home for a bite of lunch. Why don't you join me?"

"I didn't realize you had already moved in, or I would have called you before we came." She could smell the strong fragrance of a woodsy aftershave, but this time it was coming from Ethan himself. He was standing in the doorway of the bathroom, trapping her inside.

"You don't have to call ahead. It's your house, too, you know."

"It certainly doesn't feel like it belongs to me."

He began taking off the white lab jacket covering

163

his street clothes, and tossed it casually on the newly made bed.

A protest was on the tip of her tongue, but that would have sounded too familiar, too wifely. He took out his comb and ran it carelessly through his naturally curly hair. His efforts were mostly in vain, for the tight curls had a mind of their own.

Watching him perform this intimate grooming task was too much for Beth. "If you'll excuse me, please, I'll see what you have for lunch. I know the children will be hungry. I'm not."

"Surely you can eat a sandwich. There's plenty of stuff. Don't forget the chips."

Don't forget the chips. What does he think I am, a catering service? She grumbled all the way to the kitchen, but a tingling feeling persisted.

They were seated around the old claw-foot table in the dining room, once again a pseudofamily, with only Granny missing. The children were delighted Ethan had appeared and regaled him with their recent farm adventures. Ethan was very attentive and laughed at their stories in all the right places.

He does know how to handle the children, she thought ruefully, *and he does seem to like them*. They obviously adored him, vying for his attention. Beth made sure that her part of the conversation was light and carefree. Things were going along very well until Ethan spoke to her.

"Have you heard anything about your new job?"

Both children looked at her in puzzlement. Beth shot him an angry look. "There's nothing to tell. Everything is just fine. Do you children want to eat some ice cream out on the porch?"

"Okay," said Cally. "Can we have some cookies, too?"

Beth would have promised them almost anything just to get them away from the table, and she quickly dipped up their bribe.

164

Once they were settled, she returned to the table.

"Sorry. I thought they knew." Ethan was truly contrite.

"I decided not to tell them until there was something to tell. There's no sense in getting them all upset over a possibility."

"*Have* you heard anything?" he persisted.

"I had an interview." She began clearing away the lunch dishes. "I'm supposed to hear tomorrow." She tried to sound casual.

"You really do want that job, don't you?" Ethan was watching her face carefully, as if trying to read her thoughts.

She faced him squarely. "Yes, I think I do. It's time for a change in my life."

"Are you still having the bad dreams?" he asked softly.

"Not often, now that I'm jogging." She had tried hard to lock him out of her life, but it was difficult because he knew so much about her. And here he was again, crashing in.

"I was afraid Granny's death might stir up some bad feelings." He put out his hand to take hers, halting her cleaning of the table. "Are you really all right, Beth?"

The timbre of his voice stopped Beth's heart for several beats, and she held her breath.

"I'm fine, Ethan," she said, giving him a firm answer.

Ethan continued to hold her hand, searching her face, until a call from the other room shattered their trance.

"Mom, can we go down to the lake?"

Beth wanted them to leave—maybe the long waiting was over. She wanted them to stay—she was afraid to find out. Only Ethan could decide the issue.

"I must get back to my office." Quickly he rose and hurried to retrieve his lab coat, stopping at the front door to call out, "I'm on my way. Thanks for the good lunch. I'll call you tomorrow night." And he was gone.

Beth held her tears until the children scampered across the lawn to feed the ducks on the lake. Then she cried, her tears falling into the soapy dishwater. "Why does he run from me every time things begin to get tense?" She held up a plate and talked to her reflection. "You never get close enough to him to confront him and find out what's going on." She paused. "But you're to the point of doing just that." After a moment of consideration, she conceded, "No. No, you wouldn't."

Miserably she put the dishes away. *If only I could get that job, everything would be all right. Please, God, let me get the job. Please.*

The day crept by slowly, filled with almost unbearable tension. Everything seemed to hinge on Beth's getting the job, and she prayed for it off and on all day. When bedtime finally came, she tucked the children in and settled down to watch the late show on television. It was an old movie, poignant with unrequited love and missed opportunities. She found herself weeping heartily with the heroine when all seemed lost. Yet she knew there would be a happy ending, and, when it came, she felt lonelier than ever. *Too bad life isn't like a two-hour movie.* The clock struck one o'clock and Beth gave up her blues and went to bed.

The blue turned to black as she suffered the same disturbing dream again. Only this time Granny and Ethan were were her as well. When she awoke and recovered from the fright, she recalled wryly, *At least this time there was a variation on the old theme. Pretty soon the script will probably include a cast of thousands!*

Since it was nearly dawn, Beth chose to stay awake rather than chance a sequel to the nightmare. She

166

followed her usual routine and made coffee to be drunk outside in the swing under the hackberry tree. It was muggy and sticky, but she sat where she could hear the first sounds of the awakening earth. It was calming to hear the first of the mockingbirds staking out their territory. The two squirrels that lived in the old purple martin bird apartment scampered out, at times flying from limb to limb in their search for a safe way to the ground. When they sensed danger, they froze so effectively that Beth lost sight of them until they began to move again. Between the humidity and the hot coffee, Beth was growing decidedly warm. *Time for a quick shower*, she thought, *and a long wait*.

She waited until after three-thirty, reluctant to leave the house even though she had some errands she could have run to shorten the day. It was customary for most summer school offices to close at four on the dot. *Maybe I misunderstood. Maybe I was supposed to call them. No, Kevin distinctly said he would call me.* Still, she had to fight the temptation to pick up the phone and end her wait.

I didn't get it, she thought miserably when the four o'clock deadline arrived. *But he said he would let me know one way or the other.* Surely something had happened to delay the call. *He had no news. That's why he didn't call.* Now she must endure another day like the one she had just survived. She was relieved, but not surprised, that Ethan had failed to call, too.

The next day she made it until one o'clock and then decided to give Kevin a call. *Maybe he lost my number or something*, she reasoned.

"I'm sorry, Dr. Todd is in a conference just now and cannot be disturbed. Do you wish to leave your name and number?" The secretary dutifully took the information, promising to give it to Dr. Todd as soon

167

as he was available. Taking some decisive action helped a little, but not much.

At two the phone rang.

With a trembling hand, Beth picked up the receiver and said in a firm voice, "Hello."

"Hi, Beth. Sorry I didn't call you yesterday, but to be honest, we had a hard time choosing between you and Mitch. We had to meet again this morning before we could reach a final verdict."

Beth's upper lip was getting damp during Kevin's apology. "It's all right, Kevin. I know how those things can go." Suddenly weak-kneed, she sat down in the chair beside the phone, mentally willing him to cut short the amenities.

"It's yours, Beth," he said. "We want you to come the first weekend in August. Of course, you can come sooner, but that's the official date to begin your duties. You still want the job, don't you? . . . Beth?"

"Sorry, Kevin. I'm just trying to catch my breath. I've been praying so hard that the job would come through."

"Just consider me the messenger boy."

"You know what I mean. Thanks, Kevin."

"In all fairness, you must know that I didn't try to sell you to Roger and the others. I presented your credentials. It was your interview with Roger that pretty well cinched it in his mind. We have a few old codgers on the board who still feel that ladies belong behind school desks, not in the principal's office. Once they meet you in person, though, you'll have them eating out of your hand."

"Let's hope so," she laughed.

"See you soon. Cheerio."

"Cheerio," she echoed Kevin's usual sign-off, then hung up the phone and danced around the room, hugging herself with joy.

"What's all the racket?" Sean was wide-eyed

seeing his mother in such a state. Beth grabbed him and danced him around the room, too.

"Go get Cally. We're going to have a family meeting right away."

Sean scurried off, leaving Beth to think how she was going to tell the children about her decision.

She sat down at the table and waited impatiently for Sean and Cally to appear.

"Hurry, Cally! Mom wants us for another family meeting!" She could hear Sean's urgent summons and she smiled. Family meetings had always been their method of dealing with Big Events in their lives.

"What is it, Mom? What's the Big Event this time?" Cally asked a little fearfully. Both children sat down immediately.

"We are about to start a brand-new adventure."

"Are you and Ethan getting married?" asked the preceptive Cally hopefully.

Beth laughed, "No, darling. But this is something really grand. I got a new job today."

"Are you going to be the principal at my new school now?" Sean had asked her about that many times, thinking how great it would be to have the most important person in his school be his very own mom.

"No, the job I have is in another city."

"Will it take you long to get there every day?" Sean was aware that many children were bused from their homes to the schools to which they were zoned.

"No." Things were not going quite the way she had expected. "We're going to move to another city and start everything over fresh and clean. We'll get a new house and a new school and—and everything."

The children's sober faces told her this wasn't good news at all. "I wish I could make you understand how important this is to me. I've been praying very hard for this job, and now I have it. I want you to be excited with me." She looked at their drooping mouths and sad eyes, and gathered them into her

169

arms. Nuzzling Cally's soft cheek, she said, "I guess it's too much of a shock for you to be joyful yet. But just wait until we get our new house. You can help me choose it and decorate your rooms the way you want!" There were tentative smiles at the last announcement.

"Could we get a house with a swimming pool?" asked Sean.

"Hmm, I doubt that, but maybe our house will be close enough to a pool so that you could walk there anytime you like."

"Okay, I'll try to be happy with you, Mom. Maybe it just takes time." Sean's manly attempt at bravery touched Beth deeply, and she recalled another face— with Sean's long-lashed dark eyes, his straight nose, his tilted smile. And still another, superimposed over the first—with blue eyes that crinkled at the corners, and a red-gold beard . . .

"Yes, my darling," she sighed. "It just takes time."

CHAPTER 10

IT WAS LATE in the evening when Ethan called. This time, Beth was glad to hear from him, for she had good news.

"Oh, Ethan, I got it! I got the job! I'm so happy I could die."

"Well, then, I'm happy for you."

"Could you manage to sound a wee bit more cheerful?" she chided.

"It's going to be very lonely around here without you and the children. I'm going to miss all of you." There was a definite note of longing in his voice.

"It's only a forty-five-minute drive. You can come for a visit." Irritation filtered through her happiness. If he were going to miss them so much, why hadn't he been more open about it? Why wait until now to tell her? "I wish people wouldn't wait until someone is leaving to say how much they're going to be missed."

"I have no claim on your family, so it wouldn't be fair for me to say anything one way or the other. You have to make up your mind about what's best for you and your kids."

It was true, but he didn't sound convincing. He was clearly disappointed that she was leaving, and that made her both happy and angry. He could have said something a long time ago. There had been plenty of opportunities.

"We'll have to have a going-away party. When do you leave?"

"I don't have to be in the office until the first of August, but I'll have to find a place for us to live first. And I'll have to sell this house and make arrangements to keep Granny's house clean." Things would be more complicated now, but she welcomed the challenge.

"You sound so excited. I'm glad for you, Beth."

She refused to listen to the sadness she perceived in his words. He'd had his chance and he'd thrown it away. She wasn't going to play his silly games anymore. "I *am* excited. This is my chance to leave behind all the sad things in my life." There—that ought to let him know she was serious about starting all over.

"I hope you can do just that. I'll call you later in the week. Maybe we can all go to the lake once more before you leave."

"We'll try. Thanks for calling. Good night." She replaced the receiver, feeling guilty, for she wanted to start cutting the strings of her ties with him right away.

As she lay in her bed that night, she tried to reconstruct her relationship with Ethan. What had gone wrong? First, he had been her doctor, then her counselor, and then he had become her friend. She knew he cared for her, but it had to be only as one human being cares for another. He had kissed her, had even seemed to desire her, but he had never gone beyond an imaginary line that he had drawn. He liked being with the children, but didn't want them for his own. "I enjoy stirring them up and then giving them back when they're dirty or cross," he had said that day they had all gone to the lake.

She sighed and allowed herself the luxury of shedding a few tears for a man who could never be a real part of her life. *He wants to stay on the edge of it, taking only the good parts. True, he is on call when I need him, but he acts only in an official capacity. So why do I love the guy?* she thought in confusion.

Rolling over on her back, she projected his image on the ceiling above and began to catalog Ethan's virtues. His strength of character—never leaving her in doubt as to where he stood on any issue. His good looks—just short of handsome: the eyes, the mouth, the rusty beard, the solidness of his body, those wonderful healing hands. His love for people. *Except he doesn't love me the way I want him to.* Another tear tickled its way down the side of her nose and then to the pillow where it left a damp spot. She reached for a tissue and blew her nose.

Of course, not everything about him was positive. *He is so set in his ways.* She wrinkled her nose. *I've never met a man who stayed so aloof. But when he decided only to be my friend, then that's what I guess I'll always be. He seems to have a secret game plan for his life, and no matter how I've tried, I haven't been able to do anything about that. But I do intend to alter the game plan of my life.* New resolve filled her.

"I can't change you, but once I leave here, I can remove you from my life, Ethan Stewart," she warned. Firmly she clicked off the light and settled down for the night. "And I won't dream about you tonight, either."

And she didn't.

The next morning when Beth awakened, she realized that it was Saturday and she had missed Wednesday's choir practice. "I wonder what we're supposed to sing tomorrow?" She debated the idea of staying away from church or trying to fake her way through a song with which she was unfamiliar. All day she kept putting off a decision. Late in the evening, Ethan made it for her.

"Beth," he said over the phone, "why don't we get out the boat after church and have another picnic at the lake? I'll be glad to pick you and the children up for church. We could make a day of it."

Her initial reflex was to say no, but she had promised him one more trip. The children would have such a good time. Just remembering how excited they had been the last time made it impossible to refuse him. "All right, Ethan. Yes—to both. I'll be singing in the choir, so maybe you'd let the children sit with you."

Ethan said gently, "This is the first Sunday without Granny, and it's going to be hard for all of us. Don't worry about a thing. I'll take care of Cally and Sean. And," he said in a grandiose gesture, "I'll even take care of all the food! All you'll have to do is bring suits and towels for the three of you."

"Wait a minute. Do you have any mothers-in-waiting?"

"Yes, but they'll be waiting for several more months," he chuckled. "Don't worry, I'll show up—and on time. You'll see."

As punctual as the swallows returning to Capistrano, Ethan was at their door Sunday morning.

"I'm impressed." Beth matched Ethan's bright smile with one of her own. The children swarmed Ethan and hugged him mightily.

"We're off!" He seemed almost as excited as Cally and Sean.

Later, from Beth's vantage point in the choir loft, she watched the little scenario with her children and Ethan. He had seated one child on either side of him. Cally was snuggling against him, and he smiled down at her as he put his arm around her. Sean had an enormous grin on his face, sitting proudly erect, cradling a hymnbook in his hands. Only she and Granny were missing from the family portrait, and her throat ached so that she wasn't sure she would be able to sing.

She listened carefully to the sermon, waiting to see if God was going to use the minister to shed any light on the problems still facing her in her decision to move. He spoke of patience, endurance—as in running a race—trust. All these things spoke to Beth's heart. She had been busy making out a plan for her life, praying that she was doing the right things. Now God seemed to be saying that, He, too, had a plan for her life and that He was unfolding it a day at a time for her. Silently she promised to pray continuously for patience, endurance, and trust as she lived His plan.

After church they went back to Beth's to change into their swimsuits, and then headed for the lake. Ethan was particularly cheerful, continually entertaining the children with silly jokes and songs. Beth couldn't remember ever having laughed so much. She relaxed and let Ethan take total responsibility for the day.

"First we eat, then we boat." He issued the command with mock military cadence. At the children's request, they stopped to picnic at the same spot they had used before and the cloth was spread in no time. Eating and clean-up were also achieved in record time, and they were off, speeding across the sparkling water.

The hot July day was crystal-clear, and the wind off the water kept the temperature from being uncomfortably hot. Beth savored the fine spray of tiny droplets from the lake, and the warmth of the sun penetrated her tense muscles.

With the children at the front of the boat, she and Ethan enjoyed a degree of privacy.

"How are you coming with your plans?" Ethan's beard was dewed and gleaming in the sunlight.

"I mailed my resignation and called the real estate agent to put my house on the market."

"Two big steps, huh?"

"Very. It's funny; I always think of myself as a grown-up, but taking on these new responsibilities was frightening." She grinned. "Maybe growing is a continuous process."

"Would you like some company when you start looking for a new house? I have a little experience in that area."

He looked so eager to be helpful, to be needed, that she couldn't refuse. "Sure. Next week?"

"I can work that out." He was wearing his favorite T-shirt emblazoned with the motto "Say Ah-h-h-h-h to Life," illustrated by an enormous open mouth. He had been know on occasion to wear the shirt under his doctor's white coat and flash it to a frightened child to ease the small patient through an examination. *He's not a stuffy man.* She grinned at the surprise some parents must have registered at the unorthodox practice of this wonderful man.

And he definitely was a *man*, for she had caught the admiring glances he had given her, since she had donned the emerald green suit. It was modest, but it didn't hide her charms. On the other hand, she, too, was aware that Ethan's casual dress provided her with the reminder of his utter maleness.

They tooled around the lake, feeling in complete harmony with their surroundings and each other, smiling easily. Again, Ethan allowed each child to steer the boat. Then he pulled Beth on water skis behind the boat, and the children laughed gleefully at her comical wipe-outs. It was one of the nicest days

176

Beth could remember, and she stored the memory away carefully to be taken out and enjoyed later.

As darkness began to close in, they put away the skis and puttered around the lake, watching lights flicker on in the homes along the edges. Their watery reflections reminded Beth of surrealistic Christmas trees. She shivered slightly and Ethan stripped off his shirt for her to wear. The shirt was still warm from his body heat and held his special aftershave scent. She protested, but he said, "I have an extra one in the car. I'll be fine."

When they reached shore, Ethan built a fire in the outdoor fireplace set up for cooking. Immediately the children began roasting marshmallows, laughing as they got their fingers and faces sticky with the gooey blobs of melted sugar. They seemed determined to consume the entire bag.

"Good thing we have a doctor close by," Beth remarked as she watched them.

Ethan settled down beside her, smiling at the children's sugary orgy. "I'll have to check my medical books to see what treatment to use when a child overdoses on sweets." He grinned widely. "It's probably listed under 'Mother-love and Cuddling.'" A great sigh escaped him. "I'm really going to miss these good times."

"I'm sure we will, too." Hers was a cautious reply.

His blue eyes glowed dark in the firelight, and she held her breath when he took her hand in his. "I know you're doing what you think is best for you and the children. But if you change your mind, you can always come back here." He lifted her hand to his lips and gently kissed the fingertips. His eyes were liquid and searching as he bent to her mouth and pressed her lips with his. His beard was soft against her face. He ended the kiss and quickly claimed another, this time more intimate and demanding.

177

"Ethan . . . the children," she murmured against his mouth.

"Don't worry about them. They're busy."

She could feel his arms pulling her closer, feel the warmth of him through his own shirt which she was wearing. He nuzzled his beard against her, soft and manly at the same time—a portrait of the man himself. Then, sighing, he began to pull away from her and she felt her heart follow him. "It must be time to go home."

"Ethan, wait." Her heart was banging in her chest, both from the feelings he stirred and from the fear of confrontation that was about to take place. His face looked drawn and she had the distinct feeling that he was battling with her. Softly she asked, "Why do you pull away from me every time? Is it me? Something I've done?"

Something in his eyes closed against her, shutting her out. "Yes and no, but this is not the time to talk about it." Seeing the hurt in her eyes, he added gently, "Beth, you'll just have to trust me. I'm sorry." He moved away from her to rise, ending the discussion.

Misery and anger struggled for the upper hand in her heart. Anger won out. "Don't worry about it," she said in a flippant voice, erasing the moments completely. To the children, she called, "Come on, guys. It's time to go home."

Ethan put out the fire in the fireplace, and as far as she was concerned, the one in her heart—for the last time. They cleaned up the area and loaded everything into the car while he trailered the boat. She was careful to stay as far from him as possible, making plain her indifference to him.

On the way home, the children provided the small talk, and she joined in to show Ethan she was not in the least affected by what had happened between them.

When they reached the house, Beth got the children out of the car quickly and said to Ethan as she shut the door, "Thank you for a memorable day."

His face was a study in resignation.

As she dressed for bed and turned off the light, she added a last thought. "And that, my friend, is *that*."

She didn't know why Ethan continued to hover just at the fringes of her life, but she had finally come to terms with it. It was his problem now, not hers. No more abortive love scenes. No more tears. It was a promise to herself that she firmly intended to keep, and she would be careful never again to put either of them in an awkward situation.

"Dearest Granny," she whispered to the night, "your little plan didn't work. I'm so sorry for all of us."

The next day Beth made an extensive list of all the things that had to be done before they would be ready to move. She fought momentary panic, knowing everything had to be completed before the first of August. The most pressing problem was finding a place to live.

A call to the real estate man netted her an appointment for the next day to look at prospective homes. Remembering her promise to Ethan, she called his office, too, and arranged for him to go with her. Their conversation was friendly and brief, with neither of them mentioning the unfortunate ending to their day together.

The time spent with the realtor was fruitless.

"I can't believe everything is so expensive," she complained as they drove around her prospective new community. "When I look at the small lots these houses have been built on, I realize that Granny's property must be worth a small fortune."

"*Our* property," Ethan corrected her. He was quiet

for a while and then said, "Would it help if we sell it? You could use the money."

The generosity of his offer stunned her. "Sell Granny's house? Ethan, I wouldn't dream of it. I couldn't stand the thought of anyone else's living there. I just couldn't." She turned to him. "But it was wonderful of you to offer."

"I want you happy, Beth, and I'll do what I can to make that happen."

"Thank you," she said simply, accepting what he said as true.

They left the city, finding nothing suitable, but the realtor promised them more houses to look at the next day.

"I know you can't take off two days in a row, and maybe a lot more. I'll come back by myself." She read a look in his eyes. "Don't worry, I'm a big girl. I can take care of myself. And," she added, "if I can find anything, I'll show it to you first before I buy it. You can check out the plumbing and the electrical system."

"Thanks, I think. It doesn't hurt to have two people look over a house."

Two people. Beth remembered the awkwardness of explaining to the agent that she was buying the house, and, no, they weren't planning to be married. It still rankled her to remember his flat statement: "You'll have a harder time qualifying for a loan as a single woman. Better marry him and make it easier for all of us."

But she grinned when she remembered his next statement and the look on his face at their reaction. "Maybe you could buy the house together. Joint ownership is a new thing, but it's bound to become popular." She and Ethan hadn't been able to restrain their laughter.

Beth worked hard the next few days, marking one item after another off her long list. She found two houses that she felt fit her needs and her pocketbook. Ethan approved of them, too.

She and Ethan were spending a lot of time together, but it was easy companionable time. She kept her promise to herself not to expect anything more from Ethan than his friendship. He was delightful to be with, charming and witty. Only when he accidentally brushed her hand or took her arm to guide her, did the old feelings surface. She quelled them immediately. It was too pleasant being with him to let anything spoil it again.

When she went to bed at night, she thanked God for providing someone like Ethan to help her through the trying days. The pressure was building to get everything done, and there was still so much left.

She was grateful to God, too, that her bad dreams, and her good ones, seemed to have disappeared. Occasionally, the remnants of one stayed with her as she awoke. She tried to keep up with her jogging schedule and was fairly successful. Since she was leaving she had stopped going to choir practice, but she attended church regularly with Ethan. She knew people must be speculating on their relationship; however, she didn't feel the need to explain it.

She felt in charge of her emotions about Ethan. That didn't stop the heartache when she saw the children with him. They were squeezing out every ounce of love from their contact with him, knowing that soon he would be out of their lives. They had accepted the inevitability of the move, were even excited about it, but they lived only in the present—and Ethan was their present.

Beth's present was becoming one of constant tension. There were nights, despite her activities and jogging, when she was too tired to sleep. She was also too tired to fight back memories. In the daytime she could reason away the disappointment of their relationship. At night alone in her bed, Ethan's touch came back to haunt her. Sometimes it got all muddled with feelings of anger toward Robert for not being there. If he were still alive, there would be no anguish over Ethan. And where was Granny when she needed her? Safe and peaceful in the arms of her Savior.

Of course, Beth was aware, God had been good in giving her the job she longed for so desperately, but other needs were unfulfilled. Perhaps God had all that waiting for her in the near future. Maybe that's why she had gotten the job. Surely that must be the answer. She tried to rest on the last thought. *They call that Hope*, she thought as she drifted off into dreamless sleep.

CHAPTER 11

ONLY SIX MORE DAYS *until we actually pack and move to the new house.* Beth was surveying the large walk-in closet in her bedroom and thought of all the years' accumulation in the children's bedrooms. *I should have gotten rid of two-thirds of that stuff before now.* Now she didn't even have the children to help her. Her mother and father had begged for equal time with Cally and Sean, and it had been impossible to deny them, lest she be accused of playing favorites with the Martins.

She was uneasy with the children away. *They need to be here to experience this transition with me.* But what she wanted for them couldn't always be managed. Dispiritedly she shut the door to the closet and gave up trying to make heads or tails out of the impossible job of sorting through and disposing of the cast-off items.

Beth's bedroom looked like the setting for a disaster movie, for all the boxed things from her office at school were stacked around the room.

Hands in the pockets of her blue jeans, she strolled

into Sean's deserted room. There was a small box open on his bed. Idly she fingered the contents—a favorite car, some marbles, his jackknife, an old picture of his dad, some baseball cards. She recognized them at once as his prized possessions, carefully packed. He had written his name on the outside of the box. *It looks like we're moving. He's all ready to go. I wish it were that easy for me.* She dreaded the emotional uprooting as much as the physical, and she knew there would definitely be many adjustments to make when they started their new life.

The challenge Kevin had offered her was one she was eager to meet. There was no doubt that she was capable of rising to that challenge, but the worst part was the waiting; there was much that had to come before she got to the satisfying part.

Picking up the phone, she dialed her parents' number only to get no answer. *Mom and Dad are knocking themselves out to entertain the children, I'll bet.* Punching the button to disconnect the number, she automatically began dialing Granny. *What in the world are you doing?* she scolded herself.

A wave of homesickness swept over her. Beth sorely missed Granny's homespun way of putting things into perspective. But Granny wasn't home. It was now Ethan's number. For a moment, she was tempted to call him. There would be nothing wrong with that. She prowled around the room arguing with herself and finally went back to the phone. *Maybe he'll invite me to dinner, or maybe I could cook for us.* After the fifth ring she hung up. *Where is everyone when I need them?* Filled with self-pity, she resorted to her time-honored way of dealing with disappointment. She took a leisurely hot bath.

Soaking in the scented water, she thought long and hard about the things that were bothering her. It wasn't that difficult to figure out what was wrong. It was deciding what to do about it that was the hard part. She lay back, her head propped against the back of the tub, soothing soapsuds gently lapping against her body. It had been two long years of coping with one problem after another. Heartache had been heaped upon heartache. *I feel as though I have been pushing the proverbial rock up the hill by myself, but,* she thought with pride, *I haven't been run over by it yet.* Thinking about the new life just around the corner made her realize that she was almost to the end of her trials. *I hope so! Oh, I hope so!* With a start she realized, *What I thought I couldn't endure is almost over and I have survived and become stronger.* With that affirmation, she climbed out of the tub and dressed for bed.

Sleep came easily, but so did the dream. She awoke, almost incoherent with fear, and grabbed for the phone. "Ethan, Ethan! I can't stand any more! Please help me! Please!"

He recognized the hysteria and sought to calm her. "I'll be there in minutes. Go into the kitchen and warm some milk."

"You want me to warm milk? Ethan, I'm scared to death!"

"Do something, Beth. Keep busy until I can get there. Start a pot of coffee." And he hung up.

She sat there with the dead receiver in her hand and tried to concentrate. "Coffee. Yes, I'll make some coffee."

She had barely measured the aromatic ground coffee for the coffee maker when she heard Ethan's car in the driveway.

Throwing open the door, she fell into his arms. "It was so bad! Ethan, I feel like I'm losing my mind! Do something!"

He held her and rocked her and murmured soft words. "Beth, do you trust me?"

"Yes, of course." Her weeping had subsided to quiet tears coursing down her face.

"I don't want you to run from this. I want you to fight it out. You're doing battle with yourself right now." He led her to the softness of the velvet couch and sat down beside her.

Beth felt her body ruffled by tremors, like water when a stone is dropped on its surface.

"Tell me the dream," he urged.

Beth closed her eyes, wanting to shut out the memory, but Ethan's insistent voice propelled her into its black depths. "I'm in an important building—" her words betrayed her bewilderment—"but I don't know why it's important. I'm looking for someone, someone who has made me very angry. I must confront him, but I'm afraid of him. The building is empty. There are no furnishings—only cold, bare walls. At the far end of the building I see a light and I quietly move toward it. I know the man is powerful, but I'm so angry with him that I have to find him, to make him listen to me. I'm barefoot and the floor feels cold and damp as I move toward him. I can see him now, and I'm getting close enough to see that he is turned away from me." Beads of sweat popped out on her forehead as her inner eyes led her deeper into the nightmare. "My mind is very clear. He has to listen to me, to correct some wrong."

Her hand reached for Ethan's and squeezed it unmercifully. "And then without warning I'm in the top of this building, like a balcony, and the entire place is on fire. The man is standing below me, watching. He knows I'm trapped, but he does nothing to save me. All around me the flames are getting closer and hotter. I scream and scream, but he just stands there and watches, his face expressionless. Oh, Ethan, why won't he help me!" She threw her arms around his neck and wept bitterly.

Ethan comforted her, cradling her head on his shoulder and rocking her gently, crooning soft sounds, and when the weeping stopped, he lifted her

186

chin to look into her swollen face. "I told you the first time I saw you in my office that you were angry. All that anger was finally too much to keep inside. It takes enormous emotional energy to bottle it up. And now that you can plainly see that anger, you need to deal with it."

Beth was too tired to struggle. "All right. I know I'm angry. But who is the man in my dream? Do you think it's Robert?"

His eyes measured her face. "Do you?"

She moved out of the circle of his arms and stood, pacing her agitation at his question. She stopped and turned to him, looking so vulnerable in her soft cotton robe, her face that of a lost child. "If it isn't Robert, then who is it?"

Ethan asked softly, "Who do you know who is so powerful that he has control over your life—and death?"

Every muscle in her body froze, leaving her a living statue. Through stiff lips came only one word. "God." Suddenly she seemed to melt before him, and Ethan sprang to steady her swaying body. He eased her back to the couch. Her face was pale, but resolute. "People who get mad at God go to hell."

"When Jacob wrestled with God, all he got was a funny thigh bone." He wasn't exactly smiling, but Beth saw a glimmer in his eye.

"You think it's okay to be mad at God," she said flatly.

"As long as you make up with Him."

She massaged her forehead, trying to ease the chaos in her mind. "Ethan, I want you to go. My mind feels like a blender." Quickly she added, "I'm not unhappy with you, I just need some time to sort all this out."

"If later you do find out you were mad at me, too, I forgive you in advance."

Her smile was crooked. "You make me feel like

I'm on a skateboard. I've never met anyone like you."

He rose and moved toward the door. With his hand on the doorknob, he turned. "People who wrestle with God may know Him best. Fight with Him, Beth, and let Him come to you in all His love." The door clicked softly behind him.

Sitting for a moment, she weighed his words. Then she headed for her place of refuge, the gigantic old hackberry tree.

She looked up into the tree, noting the tiny stars that flickered in and out behind the barely moving black leaves. Only the sound of the crickets broke the heavy silence. It was as if God were waiting for her to speak first.

She chose a place at the foot of the tree, leaning back into the massive base. Huge limbs formed an umbrella over her head, thousands of leaves hanging limply in the stillness.

"God," she whispered to the vastness of the night sky, "I feel as though You are as far away from me as those stars. All my life I've believed in You and trusted You to take care of me. I knew whatever happened was part of Your plan. But when You took Robert from me, You almost killed me. For two long years I've waited for the peace You promise the ones who love You." Angry tears choked her to a whisper. "Where is that peace, Lord? I thought maybe it might come with a new love when I met Ethan. Instead, I have a doctor who wants to cure me, not a man to love me. Wasn't it enough to take Robert from me? Must You deny me Ethan's love, too? Then Granny came into my life. She was so wise and caring. I needed her. Now *she's* gone. Why?" Her voice rose stridently in anger. "What do You want from me? I know I haven't been as faithful as I should have, but I won't make any deals with You." Her chin jutted stubbornly. "I know You're still there. Why won't

You help me?" Softly she moaned, "I need You. Where are You? Please come back. Let me feel Your love again. Your hand is so heavy on me. Take it away before I break." She hugged her knees to her chest, feeling the physical pain of sorrow crushing her. "Ethan was right. I *am* mad at You. You're the One with all the power. You can make things work out any way You want them. Why won't You let me have a man's love? Do you want me to devote myself only to You?" She stopped short with this new thought. "Is that what You want from me?"

Suddenly subdued, she prayed again: "Lord, heal my anger." A piece of one of the Psalms flitted through her mind. "And wash my iniquities." She turned her tearstained face to the stars once more. "Help me, God."

She flinched as something brushed against her. No one was there, but she distinctly felt a touch. Then the young saplings in the corner of the yard began bending, bowing in the windless night. Hope blossomed in her heart like a tiny popcorn seed, swelling to bursting, exploding into full joy. There was no doubt about it. The Lord had come to her! Peace flooded her, washing away the anger and disappointment. "You *are* here. You *do* love me," she whispered as her skin prickled in wonder. "Granny was right! It's all right to fight with You. I've battled with You and You still love me."

It was almost too much for her mind to grasp. Even with Robert and Ethan gone from her life, something was waiting— something wonderful. She had only to rest in peaceful joy until the Lord revealed His plans for her. And, strangest of all, Beth realized she was not even in a hurry to know what they were.

She walked back into the house and crawled into bed. Sleep came instantly—quiet, gentle sleep. Everything was going to be all right. The Lord was with her.

The insistent ringing of the phone woke her. She knew before she reached for it that Ethan would be on the other end of the line.

"Beth, are you all right?" His anxiety came over the phone clearly.

"Yes, I'm fine. Thank you for coming last night."

"You sound so far away. Are you sure you're okay?"

"Ethan, something important happened to me last night. Something I'm not ready to share just yet. Give me a few days to think. I'll call you when I'm ready to talk."

Reluctantly he agreed. "But don't hesitate to call me, day or night, when you do decide."

"Yes, of course. Don't worry," she insisted. "I'm fine." She placed the receiver back into its cradle and stretched luxuriously. She was not only fine, she felt wonderful. Ethan's voice had not set in motion the adolescent waves of anxiety she had experienced before. She accepted the fact that he was checking on an hysterical patient, and thanked God that she had such a good and caring doctor. *Mine even makes housecalls in the middle of the night*, she marveled.

The next few days were spent basking in her new-found relationship with God. Thoughts of Him and prayerful meditation dominated her days. She felt whole again, healed after a long two-year illness. She was still awed by her experience and relived the coming of the wind over and over in her mind, the newness of it never diminishing.

She was also able, at last to deal with her nightmare. In the light of day she took each part and carefully examined it. Talking aloud to herself, she listed the symbols.

"I've heard that the dreamer is the only one who knows what each element in the dream stands for. What could the important building be? It's built of

190

stone, has oddly shaped windows, and someone important lives there." She sat still for a moment trying to reconstruct the building in her mind. It stayed just beyond her mental reach, so she found a pad and pencil and tried to sketch out the general shape. After only a few strokes, the rude outline of a cathedral—a church—was evident.

A wave of anxiety swept over her as she instantly realized who the important person must be. "It has to be God," she whispered. But her mind rebelled, for the God in her dreams had been uncaring. "Is that what I thought about God?"

Yes, she had to admit it was. God had done nothing to stop Robert's death, leaving her with pain and sorrow. "God, forgive me for thinking of You as uncaring." And the tears flowed freely as she relived those feelings—and began to piece together the meaning of her terrifying dreams. "I must be going to church to confront You, to make You give Robert back to me. But even in my dream I know how powerful You are. I see You turn Your back on me. O dear Lord, that's how it felt then." She wiped the tears from her face with the back of her hand and plunged on.

"When I find myself on the balcony, I'm even farther away from You and then You punish me with the fire. The fires of hell?" Another chilling thought sprang into her consciousness. "Or am I punishing myself because I know that what I'm thinking is wrong?" She felt dazed as she tried to weave her way through the tangled threads of her thoughts.

"I go to God for help. I think He is turning His back on me, and isn't helping me even when I'm in danger. And because I have had such sinful thoughts about God, I am punishing myself." Could it be that simple? A terrible dream that had plagued her for so long, broken down into concrete terms, seemed too simplistic to account for all her suffering.

"Yet it does all fit. I did feel that way. How mad I was at You, God, for letting all that happen to me." She closed her eyes in acceptance. "I don't understand, but I am grateful you didn't abandon me in my great anger. Thank You for letting me struggle with You and finally come to terms with all this. I know You love me." By now the tears of repentance had become tears of happiness and overwhelming love. "Ethan was right, Lord, from the very start."

With the relief of her new-found knowledge came overpowering fatigue, and putting down her head, she slept a deep, body-restoring sleep.

Awaking with her mouth curved in a gentle smile, she called the children and had a happy chat with them. There was no way she could share with them the enormous experiences she was going through, so she let them do most of the talking. She missed them, but the nagging worry over their absence was gone. She was genuinely glad they were having such an enjoyable visit.

On the fourth day of her self-imposed spiritual retreat, the doorbell rang. Beth clip-clopped to the door in her sandals. She was dressed in a bright sun dress, a reflection of her new joy.

Ethan's face looked like a forecast for rain. Worry clouded his usually bright blue eyes. "May I come in?"

"Certainly. It's nice of you to make another housecall," she teased. "Want some iced tea? I was just making some for myself."

"Yes." He followed her into the kitchen and sat down at the table, spreading his hands across the bright yellow cloth.

"Ethan, what's the matter? You look terrible."

"I've been so worried about you. Why didn't you call?" he demanded tensely.

"I didn't mean to worry you." She had never seen

192

him look so haggard—not even during Granny's ordeal.

"I was afraid I had pushed you too far the night I made you face your anger. I've imagined the worst."

She was instantly penitent. "I'm sorry. I never realized you took your responsibilities so seriously. I told you I needed time to think." Her eyes danced merrily. "You *have* lost a patient, though."

She began to relate the story of the wind to him. When she reached the part about the trees' bowing, she saw the hairs of his arms prickle in goosebumps. "You believe me, don't you," she said gratefully. "I had goosebumps all over my body. Oh, Ethan," she said exuberantly. "It was the most wonderful experience of my life. How can I ever thank you for opening that door for me?"

"By letting me in, too."

"What?" Uncertainly she set down her glass, for it had suddenly developed a pronounced wobble.

He took her newly freed hand in his large warm ones. "Beth, it's easy for a doctor to become too involved with a patient, especially one like you. You were so vulnerable. I thought my infatuation with you would fade away. But it kept growing. I thought you might be in love with me, too, especially when you called, so frightened you were incoherent. After I saw you, I knew you'd have to fight your battle to the end before you could love me fully." He stopped for breath.

"But . . ."

"Just wait and let me get through all this. I've been rehearsing it for two days." He stood and pulled her behind him as he strode into the living room. "I don't want the table between us when I talk to you." He settled them both on the couch, sitting at an angle so they faced each other. He looked into Beth's blank face, his blue eyes burning into hers, demanding that

193

she hear him out. "I can't be silent any longer. I love you, Beth. I need you. Please marry me."

Beth thought for an instant that she couldn't bear any more happiness. She moved against him into the circle of his arms. "I've wanted to do that from the first day we met. Hold me tightly and don't let go." She pressed even harder against him. "I love you, I love you. And yes, I will marry you."

He pulled away just enough to look into her shining eyes. "Beth." All the love in his heart was in that one word. His mouth moved toward her parted lips and claimed at last what he had hungered for for so long. What began as a gentle kiss grew into a sealing of their hearts.

Breathlessly she broke away. "I didn't want you to think I was just another neurotic woman patient after you, but I've loved you from the first day I saw you. But you were always so professional with me. I thought you were just a dedicated doctor." She looked at him with new wonder. "We were both so careful, we almost didn't find each other." They shared a soft laugh.

"Oh, Ethan, my new job—and the house!" Beth sat erect, suddenly aware of the implications of his proposal. "What will we do?"

"How many choices do we have?"

"Always the practical one, aren't you?" She was quiet for a moment, thoughtful. "I'd like to keep my job. I've worked hard for it." She could see Ethan concentrating on that very large problem. "But," she added, "I want to live in Granny's house."

"Can you commute to your job?" He slid his fingers softly down the side of her face.

"Yes, I think so. It really isn't so far, and a lot of people do that. It's not an ideal solution, but it's the only one I can think of right now . . . It's a little hard to concentrate with you so close," she accused, moving away slightly. "Maybe we could try it for a

194

Denver First Wesleyan Church
3440 W. Louisiana Ave.
Denver, Colorado 80219

year. If it doesn't work, perhaps I'll go back to school for my certification as a superintendent. The present one is due for retirement in a year or so.'' She grinned. ''Maybe that's why the Lord let me get that job. Maybe He had it in mind for me all the time. Do you suppose that's so?''

''With God, *anything* is possible,'' he sighed contentedly.

''Of that, I'm certain.''

''Doctor,'' she said against his searching lips, ''I'm going to take your advice and fall in love again.''

''Beth,'' he sighed, ''you'll need prolonged and extensive treatment.''

''Yes, Doctor, dear.''

So this was what she had been waiting for. With her eyes closed, she saw the young saplings bending again. But still there was no wind.

MEET THE AUTHOR

LINDA TIMIAN HERRING is a modern woman who cherishes traditional values. Having recently moved to Galveston, Texas, with her family, she delights in her roles as teacher at Trinity Episcopal School, minister's wife, and mother of four. From these diverse elements in her own life, she has crafted another compelling and hauntingly beautiful story of conflict and overcoming.

Linda is also the author of *Morning Song*, her first novel for Serenade Books.

A Letter To Our Readers

Dear Reader:

Pioneering is an exhilarating experience, filled with opportunities for exploring new frontiers. The Zondervan Corporation is proud to be the first major publisher to launch a series of inspirational romances designed to inspire and uplift as well as to provide wholesome entertainment. In order that we might better contribute to your reading enjoyment, we would appreciate your taking a few minutes to respond to the following questions and return to:

> Anne Severance, Editor
> 1415 Lake Drive, S.E.
> Grand Rapids, Michigan   49506

1. Did you enjoy reading WINDSONG?

   ☐ Very much. I would like to see more books by this author!
   ☐ Moderately
   ☐ I would have enjoyed it more if _____

2. Where did you purchase this book? _____

3. What influenced your decision to purchase this book?
   ☐ Cover   ☐ Back cover copy
   ☐ Title   ☐ Friends
   ☐ Publicity   ☐ Other _____

4. Please rate the following elements from 1 (poor) to 10 (superior).

☐ Heroine   ☐ Plot
☐ Hero   ☐ Inspirational theme
☐ Setting   ☐ Secondary characters

5. Which settings would you like to see in future Serenade books?

_____   _____

_____   _____

6. What are some inspirational themes you would like to see treated in future books?

_____   _____

_____   _____

7. Would you be interested in reading other Serenade/ Serenata or Serenade/Saga Books?

☐ Very interested
☐ Moderately interested
☐ Not interested

8. Please indicate your age range:

☐ Under 18   ☐ 25–34   ☐ 46–55
☐ 18–24   ☐ 35–45   ☐ Over 55

9. Would you be interested in a Serenade book club? If so, please give us your name and address:

Name _____

Occupation _____

Address _____

City _____ State _____ Zip _____

Serenade/Serenata Books are inspirational romances in contemporary settings, designed to bring you a joyful, heart-lifting reading experience.

Other Serenade books available in your local bookstore:

Watch for forthcoming books in both the contemporary and historical series coming soon to your local book store: